HIJACKED HITMAN

RON G. ROBERTSON

ENCHANTED INDIE PRESS

Austin, Texas

PUBLISHER'S NOTE

Copyright © 2015 by Ron G. Robertson
Cover design and interior formatting: Tosh McIntosh
Front Cover Photo © Sebastien Nasica

Printed and published in the United States of America
Enchanted Indie Press
ISBN-13: 978-1938749-27-8
ISBN-10: 1938749278

Also available in eBook
ISBN-13: 978-1-938749-28-5
ISBN-10: 1938749286

To my parents, Nila and Eugene
To Dylan, for all you've given
To Ginger, for always believing

CHAPTER ONE

*A*n unusually mild afternoon washed over Manhattan as tourists and locals strolled in Little Italy. Terraces in front of restaurants along Mulberry Street were filling up quickly. Across from Carlo's Restaurant people lounged in the sun at sidewalk tables. It seemed like a perfect afternoon until --

Pap, pap, pap, came from inside Carlo's, followed by a scream. Then a louder bang, definitely a gunshot, and more pap-paps.

Quiet followed briefly. Then boom, boom ... boom, boom.

Onlookers were stunned into silence when a little old lady bustled through the entrance from Carlo's and hurried up the street pulling a small shopping cart. A man rushing toward the restaurant was distracted by the squeaky wheel on her cart, his eyes drawn to the glint of steel and what looked like a rifle barrel poking from a box on the cart. The old lady deftly snapped a cardboard panel over the opening without pausing and continued north on Mulberry.

"They're all dead!" shouted someone stumbling out of Carlo's.

More people ran toward the restaurant as the sound of sirens grew closer.

Several minutes later the little old lady turned the corner onto Prince Street and gasped for breath. She trembled all over with the realization of what had just happened. As she stared at her reflection in a shop's window, her mind flashed from the mob boss, dead on the floor, to the faces of two young men: one locked in an Upper West Side bedroom; the other, a confused young man *climbing the stairs of an office tower downtown.*

So much had happened so fast, it seemed like another life.

Just two weeks before, Sam Robbins entered his office building feeling invigorated from the walk from his apartment in Chelsea. It wouldn't be easy to stay inside on this pleasant April day. Another boring Thursday, he figured. But he could cut out for a few minutes after 9 and do 20 or 30 flights of stairs. It was part of his fitness program and it would break up the tedium.

"Hey, Sam. How's it goin'?"

"Morning, Melvin," Sam replied mechanically, without even glancing at the smiling security guard. Sam entered the elevator, the only occupant this early in the morning, and started the long ride up. At the 47th floor, he unlocked the office area and headed straight to his desk.

"Good morning."

Christ, thought Sam. Anne-Marie Fazini, all smiles and over-rouged cheeks. "G'morning, Anne-Marie. You're up early."

"You always say that." Her fading smile seemed half-sure.

"Do I?" He gave a quick wave and brushed past.

At his desk, Sam pushed a Runner's World magazine aside and flipped the on switch for his PC.

"Hmm," he mimicked the sound of the powering-up monitor, hanging his jacket on its hook. He sat back and looked at his watch. Thirty-eight minutes. Not bad for four miles. He listened to make sure Anne-Marie had not followed him. He doubted she had any work to do all day, let alone this early. With an audible sigh, he unlocked his desk and opened the file drawer.

There was the new annual issue of Guns magazine. Sam

frowned at the cover wrinkled from yesterday morning's drizzle, and spread it on the corner of his desk near a stack of paperwork he could use to conceal it should Anne-Marie wander over. "Reviews of over 400 new handguns and rifles," he read in childlike fascination, letting his imagination run freely.

The weather didn't fully explain his restlessness. Through the unusually harsh winter, Sam had kept to his half-furnished apartment, swearing he was ready to move on after his divorce two years ago, but he continued to distance himself from friends at the office. He needed a change. And when he saw the Guns Annual on the newsstand a couple of nights ago, he couldn't resist. He was lured back into an interest he had had since childhood, the awesome power of guns. The movies and all the crap on television didn't even come close to what it must really be like to be a cop or government agent, or even a thug. And what was he doing with his life? Counting numbers for a less than exciting government bureaucracy, reassigning and keeping track of offices and goods.

He wanted, lusted for, one of those beautiful new 10mm automatic pistols. It would be expensive, but he could justify that. Even the cops told people to get a gun to protect themselves, despite what top city officials said publicly. But what would he do with it? The temptations he felt were ominous.

"Wet again, I see."

Sam whirled around at the unexpected voice, quickly covering the magazine with his arm and blocking it with his body.

"Pete!"

Peter Hankfield, Sam's supervisor, raised one bushy eyebrow.

"Easy, Sam old boy. I do come in early once in a while. What are you up to there?" Pete craned his neck with obvious delight.

"Just ... just making myself a few notes," said Sam, thinking quickly. "Call my mother, go by the cleaners ..."

"Don't forget the stairs."

"Huh?"

"The ol' exercise fanaticism. You do still run up the stairs every day, don't you?" Pete said, half sneering.

"You should try them yourself sometime, Pee-ter," Sam replied icily, emphasizing both syllables of the man's name. "You never know when you might have to. What if the power went off again? You know, no elevators for an easy ride."

"I'd sit right here until they got the damn things fixed."

"Yeah, right." Sam slowly turned back to face the computer screen. "See you, Peter." Again he emphasized the name.

Pete stared at Sam's back, then turned and walked away.

Sam forced himself into his work. Facts and figures. Dull numbers connected to dull accounts and even duller people. He was filled again with the restlessness of last night, when he had given in and slammed the video "Blue Steel" into the ancient VCR and so quickly fell into the fantasy.

Nine o'clock. Sam headed for the stairs.

The air there was warm and steamy, making him feel light-headed. After hurrying down 15 flights of stairs and starting back up again, he stood catching his breath on the landing at the 35th floor, a wide balcony-like area where one stairwell connected to another through a long hallway. Through a quirk of design, one of the building's support columns ran through just before the hallway door, forming an alcove, barely big enough for a person, that was hidden from view. Sam stood there in the shadows, waiting for his heartbeat to slow down. He ran his fingers through the dampness of his short brown hair, then skimmed them down his slim torso. It had taken several months, but he had shed the 15 pounds he'd put on right after the divorce.

He was ready to continue, but as he reached for the door, he heard footsteps.

Probably someone coming out to sneak a smoke, he thought. Sam didn't feel like greeting anyone, so he pressed back into the alcove. He would wait.

The door opened.

"You sure this is okay?" came a hoarse whisper, half-panted. "I don't like it."

"No one uses the stairs. Would you?"

"I don't even like it now. I told you."

"So talk."

"We could have just done this somewhere else."

"We're here. Tell me."

"It's April the 20th."

"Two weeks."

"At Carlo's in Little Italy. He goes for lunch every Thursday at 11:30."

"So?"

"That's the time."

"What time?"

"11, 11:30."

"Always the same?"

"Always. Unless there's some screwup and his boys get suspicious."

"Don't worry. They won't get nervous from me. You know

that."

"Yeah, well."

"How do you want it?"

"What do I care?" said the panting one, raising his voice. Then, catching himself, he added quietly, "Just get it done."

"Don't worry," the other man answered, sounding almost sad. "He'll be very dead."

"Yeah. Great. Let's get out of here."

Dead! thought Sam. What the hell was going on?

"Payment?" Sad Voice said.

"Right. Here." There was a brief shuffle followed by a papery crinkle. "You can pick up the rest later."

"Same as always. Half now and half later. Don't screw me around this time."

"Look, it only happened that once."

"I just want you to remember that I haven't forgotten. If Joey found out, it wouldn't be good for you, Barry."

"Give me a break, Will." Panter was irritated.

"I'm giving you a break. I could have taken you out right then."

"Yeah. But you need me."

There was a pause, then the sad-voiced one, Will, spoke. "Next time, then."

"Not here. I'm not coming here again."

"It worked out this time. We'll deal with the next time later."

"Not here. I don't like it."

The footsteps resumed and Sam tried to press himself into the paint. But he needn't have worried, for when the door opened, he remained completely hidden.

On impulse, Sam reached for the doorknob before the door closed and, heart pounding, he hazarded a peek.

Yes! He recognized one of them. Someone he'd seen many times around the office. The other one, the fat one in the dark suit, didn't look familiar.

What the hell was going on?

Sam waited, tense, until the two men had to be long gone. Then he crept out of the alcove and hurried down flight after flight to 27 where he took the elevator back to his floor. The word dead still echoed.

CHAPTER TWO

Thoughts raced through Sam's head as he sat at his desk. Could this be real? It was frightening, but exciting. He fidgeted with the papers on his desk and brushed aside the folder he'd carefully put in place earlier. A glint of paper caught his eye. He found himself staring at the automatic pistol on the cover of the Guns Annual. It gleamed, glossy black on a red background, four copper-tipped cartridges shining beside the thick barrel.

Sam snatched the magazine from the desk and threw it into the back of the file drawer. For a moment he stood nervously surveying his corner of the office. Was he being watched?

Wait a minute, he told himself. I didn't do anything. I was just walking on the stairs.

Got to get out of here.

Sam didn't even hear the usual friendly words spoken by Melvin, the security guard, as he hurried out of the building. Thankfully, it wasn't raining.

He walked fast, hard. For a while he didn't even think, he just went. He found himself staring into the East River. There was no one close by, just strolling couples and individuals a block or so away. Too early for most people taking lunch.

An image came to him of a scene from some movie or book. It was night and three people stood on a barge, one of them tied up. Suddenly two dark-suited men were throwing the other one overboard. With a scream and a big splash he disappeared beneath the water.

Sam swallowed. Were those guys on the stairs actually going to kill someone?

Then with a rush, Sam could feel the hard steel of a gun in his hand. An oily-skinned man with slicked-back hair knelt before him, hands tied behind his back, eyes wild and scared. Sam put the gun to the man's head.

Sam gasped. Quickly, he looked around to make sure no one was watching. It was New York. No one noticed.

The scene, the excitement, left him famished. It was a little past noon. He turned and headed back to the office.

Sam went directly to the cafeteria where he grabbed a salad, then a sandwich. For good measure he ordered fries and picked up a piece of apple pie. Normally, he had only a salad.

Bad timing. The dining room was packed. He started toward the windows scouting for a seat.

Sam almost dropped his tray. There was Sad Voice, the man from the stairs! Sam started to turn away, but something pushed him forward.

He eased toward the table where the man sat alone.

"Oh, excuse me," said Sam as he bumped the corner of the table. "I, uh, I was looking out the window."

The man was startled. "It's all right."

"Well, I'm sorry." Sam couldn't let the moment pass. "Hey, aren't you Will from -- what department is it?" he invented, extending his right hand as he set the tray down.

"Bill. Jackson," said Sad Voice, obviously not wishing to be disturbed.

"Yeah, right. Bill. Sam Robbins." Sam continued to hold out his hand. Bill hesitated but reached out. "Mind if I sit?" Sam asked. "It's pretty crowded today."

"Fine. I'm almost finished."

"No, no. I don't mean to disturb you. I can find another place." Sam smiled warmly and made to pick up his tray.

"No, it's all right," said Bill. "Sit down."

"Thanks." Sam sat and started in on the salad, though he found he was no longer hungry.

"Turning into a nice day, isn't it," he said.

Bill was distant. "Oh, yeah."

"Hey," Sam said in his most understanding voice, "I don't mean to be a pain. I know what it's like. I like to be alone, too."

Bill studied him. "Well, enjoy," he said getting up from the table.

No! Sam's mind shouted. Don't go yet.

"Wait. What's the rush?" he stumbled.

"What?"

"Oh, nothing. It's just sort of hard for me to meet people. I'm trying to work at it. You're my first ... victim." He threw out an embarrassed grin.

"I'm not so good at it myself. You're doing fine. See you around, all right?"

"Oh, sure," said Sam, rising.

"Go ahead with your lunch. Sam, was it? I've got to get back to work."

"Right." Sam had run out of stupid comments. "I'll see you," he said and watched as Sad Voice made his way through the tables.

Sam sat numbed, the sandwich untouched before him. The

crowd became like a whirl of hornets, gradually disappearing. He looked down at the tray where most of his lunch still remained. He'd blown it. For a moment he stared out the window, then stood and walked away from the table, leaving the tray behind. The food didn't seem to matter anymore.

That evening, Sam paced his small apartment. How could he be sure Bill was the guy? No, it definitely was him. The voice, the clothes, it was him. But could he have misunderstood the conversation?

"Don't be a dope," he said aloud.

Stopping in the middle of the living room, he studied his dim reflection in the front windows. You're too jumpy, he told himself. All you have to do is forget about this.

But he knew he couldn't. The possibilities were too enticing. He had to find out. He would have to form a plan of some kind. Some way to get to know Bill and find out more.

CHAPTER THREE

It was Friday. Sam had been down to the cafeteria once before, hoping to spy Bill. It was early, earlier than he'd bumped into Bill the previous day. But he didn't want to take a chance on missing him.

Still no Bill. Sam was getting more agitated by the minute. He'd better get back upstairs before -- wait. There, coming around the corner from the elevators, was Bill. Had he seen Sam? Sam ducked into the restroom.

He stayed just a moment and hurried back out. Right in front of Bill.

"Oh, sorry." He feigned surprise. "Bill. Of all people. I was just thinking about you." Suddenly he blushed. "Oh, I didn't mean --" Sam jerked a thumb toward the men's room.

Bill smiled indulgently. "You seem in a hurry. Go ahead."

In a hurry? Damn, thought Sam. I'm too obviously nervous. "No, I was just surprised to see you. I mean, bump into you. Going to lunch?"

"Here in the cafeteria, you mean?" Bill replied sarcastically.

"Well, yeah, that was dumb. Let me buy you lunch."

"No, thanks."

"Really. I'd like to. I almost knocked you down, after all." Sam paused expectantly, glancing at his watch. "I promise not to tell Preston," he grinned.

Bill cocked his head slightly, curious at the mention of his boss' name.

"All right, Sam."

Sam could tell Bill was not comfortable, but this was definite progress. His search through company organization charts might pay off. "I won't be a nuisance," he added quietly.

"Fine," Bill smiled, it seemed in spite of himself.

As they went through the line, Sam pondered what to say. He couldn't think of food, but got more than his customary salad in hopes it would put Bill at ease. Finally, they were checked out and had found a table near the windows. It was just after noon, and with such a sunny Friday, not many people were eating in today.

"How long you worked here?" Bill asked.

Sam was surprised by this sudden turn of interest, if that's what it was, but he seized upon it. "About eight years. Yourself?"

"I came here a year and a half ago." Sam knew that already.

"What'd you do before that?"

"What do you mean?"

Sam could see he had blundered and moved quickly to correct it. "Some other nonsense, just like me, huh?"

Bill stared a second and smiled. Thank goodness it worked, Sam breathed. "Anyway, it doesn't matter, does it? I've been here all this time and barely know anyone. I mean, the people I work with. And Preston. He was an intern in our department and shot up like a rocket. You probably knew that, if you're on his right side." He laughed. "I talk too much."

"No. I wondered about that guy."

"I take it you're not one of his favored ones." Sam chuckled.

"Ah, no." Bill's slight smile seemed genuine. He lowered his eyes and took a bite of rice.

"Bill," Sam chanced.

"Yeah."

"What are you doing this evening? I mean, after work. Maybe we could stop for a drink or something? After all, we share a fondness for Preston. I could tell you a few things," Sam deliberately trailed off.

"After work?"

"Yeah. Oh, sorry, it's Friday. A guy like you, you probably got plans."

"A guy like me?"

"Yeah. Nice looking, pretty cool."

Bill laughed aloud. "Pretty cool?"

Sam gave a very serious look. "No, I'm not kidding. I guess I sound stupid."

"No, it's just the crack about Friday night, big plans. Sam, I'm not exactly Prince Charming."

"Get outta here," Sam retorted, embarrassing himself.

To this they both laughed.

"What do you say?" Sam pursued. "A couple of drinks after work?"

"Oh, now it's a couple," Bill kidded.

"So, you're on?" Sam suppressed his eagerness.

"Yeah, why not?"

Yes! Sam shouted to himself. But outwardly he tried to appear more subdued. "Good," he said and smiled.

Sam tried to get Bill to choose a place, but when he continually deferred, claiming he didn't know anywhere, Sam suggested they walk down toward the harbor and picked the first likely bar he saw. It being 4 o'clock, the place was pretty quiet. Again Sam felt his way. How was he possibly going to find out anything?

"You live around here? In the city, I mean?" he ventured.

"Yeah," Bill replied. Seeing Sam was waiting for more, he added, "Little place up on 83rd."

Whoa, 83rd? thought Sam. Nice neighborhood. "West or east?"

"West. By the park."

Central Park? This guy must have a better job than he'd figured. "Yeah? I live in the Village."

"Village? Nice."

"Well, more Chelsea, actually. Not much of a place."

"Yeah. It's not easy to find something in the city."

Sam noticed Bill's eyes wandering around the bar, stopping on the clock. "Bill," he said, leaning forward, "you ever think about getting away from here?"

"This bar?" asked Bill, puzzled.

"No. I mean, away from the city. Away from New York."

"And go where?"

"Oh, I don't know. Colorado. Arizona. Maybe some other country."

Bill seemed to be studying him. "I traveled around awhile."

"Really? Where?"

Again Bill seemed reluctant. "Oh, Philly, Detroit, Kansas City. Down Florida for a while."

"What were you doing? Salesman?" Sam regretted the question as Bill stared at him.

"It was ... personnel," Bill said quietly. "Just a job." He was silent again.

Sam watched him, his pulse beginning to quicken as he pressed on. "I've been around here for, I don't know, seems like forever. Same old things, same scenery. I thought after high school I'd join the navy or travel around or something. But, my mother."

Bill was pulled back from his distraction. "Your mother?"

Sam hesitated. "She didn't want me to go off on anything crazy, she called it. Adventurous was more like it."

Bill looked down at the table. "Smart of her."

"It was?" Sam studied the man.

"Kept you from getting in trouble, probably."

"That's what she would say. But I don't think joining the army --"

"I thought it was the navy."

"Well, either one. But ..." He didn't know where to go from here.

"So what did you do?"

Maybe the guy was interested, thought Sam. "Went on to college. Got the paper. Got a job. Then ended up here. I mean, at the office," he chuckled.

Bill laughed with him. "Maybe better than working here."

"Well, I have ended up here anyway." They both smiled. On impulse, Sam said, "Hey, you got anything going? How about dinner?"

Bill's eyes seemed to light a little. "I don't know. Maybe." Then his smile faded. "I can't, Sam. Not tonight."

Why not? Sam wanted to demand. Instead he said, "Oh. Wish you could. This is nice."

Bill frowned. "This?" he waved his hand.

Suddenly, Sam was aware that the noise level had picked up

significantly in the bar. He looked around and saw quite a few people, sitting, milling about. "What? Where'd all those people come from?"

"I don't --"

"Ohhh," groaned Sam. "Happy hour."

Bill was frowning at the growing crowd.

"Let's get out of here," Sam suggested.

"Sounds good."

They walked up West Broadway, silent for several minutes. Sam cleared his throat, nervous about breaking the quiet. "Wish you could make it for dinner, Bill." Then, "You got someplace you have to go?"

Bill slowed his stride. Sam said, "I'm sorry. It's none of my business."

Sighing, Bill said, "Well, you know. You said it before. My mother."

"Your mother?" It was barely a question.

"Right. I told her I'd be by."

"Oh. Well, that's cool."

"She's got cancer."

"I'm sorry."

"Yeah."

They walked on.

"Well," Sam began, "maybe later. After you see your mom."

Bill looked a bit hopeful. "She lives out in Queens."

"Well, hey, I'm not doing anything tonight. Just come by later. Give me a call. We'll get together." He hoped he'd covered all possibilities.

"Okay," Bill said, after seeming to consider. "Sure. Let's stop in for another drink, and I'll call later."

"We could just go up to my place. I've got some beer."

"Nah. Let's go in here," Bill motioned toward a small place at the corner. "My treat."

Sam decided to take what he could.

Sam fidgeted. It was 9:30 and Bill had not called. Munching on some crackers and carrots, he thought, well, it's not so late. But he was worried, worried it wouldn't work out. He had paced, then sat, then paced again. He still wasn't sure what he was learning from Bill. He hadn't found a hint of anything about the discussion on the stairs. Was it really talk of killing someone?

He was so stupid. Ten o'clock, the guy wasn't going to call anyway. He walked across the living room to the kitchen and stopped at the counter. His eyes fell on the same Guns magazine cover. The big pistol. The talk on the stairs. Dead!

Ring!

The phone jolted Sam from his thoughts. It rang again, and a third time before he could get his wits. Quickly, he grabbed it. "H'lo?"

"Hello, Sam."

Sam could barely hear the voice. "Bill?"

"Yeah." There was static or street sounds in the background.

"You okay?"

"Yeah. Sure."

Silence.

"Well," said Sam quickly, "so, dinner?"

"Yeah, sorry, Sam. It's pretty late."

"What the hell. It's New York. Nobody goes to dinner before 10."

Bill forced a chuckle.

"Come on over, Bill. You sound bushed."

"Yeah. These visits are a bit tiring sometimes. I could use a drink."

"Okay."

"I'm at 42nd. Just came up from the subway. I'll walk down and meet you."

"42nd? Jesus, Bill. You're not going to walk down from there?"

"Why not? Nobody's going to bother me."

"No? Well, sure. Where you want to meet?"

"Pick a place," Bill said.

"Uh, there's a place," Sam stammered, "a place on Seventh not far from 23rd, but that's a long walk for you."

"Don't worry. I need the air. What's the name? I'll meet you in 20 or 30 minutes."

"Well, The Newburgh," said Sam.

"See you there." The line went dead.

Sam's pulse was pounding. He was surprised that Bill had called, but it was more than that. His nervous fear, and excitement, that Bill was wandering around at 42nd and not worrying. True there would be a lot of theater people, but --

Stop it! he told himself. Bill's coming. Make a plan.

Sam washed his face in cold water and began to calm himself. Think of a way. Have some drinks and get him to talk.

It was not hard to get Bill to drink. He was obviously unsettled. He was on his third vodka while Sam still nursed his first beer. Conversation had been light, shallow.

"So, how's your mother? Is it hard for her, the sickness?

And hard for you?"

Bill's eyes looked bleary. "It's not just that. She knows she's going to die. Hell, we're all going to die someday."

Sam waited, but Bill seemed lost in the liquor again. "You were --" he began.

"She was on my ass so long."

After a pause, Sam asked, "Tonight?"

"What? No. No, for a long time. All those years. When I was," he looked cautiously at Sam, "when I was running all over, taking those jobs around the country."

"Jobs? Oh, you mean the traveling."

"Yeah," Bill said, "the traveling. She got the cancer and she just wouldn't listen anymore. I mean, hell, Sam."

Sam's eyes widened at the sudden loudness of Bill's voice. "My old man, he was just a nobody. Two-bit runner." He lowered his voice back to normal.

Sam snapped for the waiter's attention, ordering another round as Bill continued to talk.

"My brother, what a rowdy. And I thought he was cool, of course. They both got popped," said Bill, lowering his eyes to the empty glass.

"Popped?" His face echoed the question.

"Yeah." Bill's response sounded far away. Then looking into Sam's eyes, he said, "Killed."

"Killed?" Sam replied with more amazement than he'd intended.

"By ... who knows?" Bill shook his head as if he were having trouble remembering. "Anyway," he continued quietly, "that left just me. I'm all she's got."

"Your mother."

"Yeah."

"So you're taking care of her," Sam stated.

Chuckling, Bill said, "She wanted me to get out of it. Get some respectable work." Staring at Sam, he spoke, thoroughly sober. "What the hell. She was right."

"Well, what were you doing?"

Bill looked down and half mumbled, "Nothing much. Just jobs. Traveling around."

"The personnel stuff?" asked Sam with a frown.

"Right," said Bill. "That kind of thing."

Sam knew Bill had been involved in something disreputable. But he wasn't sure how to pursue it. His cynicism faded as he watched Bill's sad face, yet a surge of fearful excitement rushed through him. Bill was talking about killing people.

The conversation Sam had overheard on the stairs made it clear the men were not discussing the first time. And he was sure they had to have been talking about a hit. But right now, Bill seemed so vulnerable.

Sam's confusion forced him to sit dumbly, but he was convinced he had to take the chance. He might not have a better opportunity.

"So you're doing these jobs -- were doing these jobs. And your mother wanted you to get out of it. Get a regular job? What do you do now? At the office?"

Dully, Bill answered, "Work with engineering. Assistant. It's not much."

"You must have made a lot of money before, then. I mean, living on Central Park."

Bill stared, noncommittal.

Sam gulped for courage. "Or are you still ... doing the other jobs?" There! He'd said it.

Bill continued to stare at him for at least a minute, then turned his attention to the moisture on the table. Sam's heart pounded. Bill's sudden movement, pushing back from the table, unnerved him.

"Let's go. I need some air," Bill said calmly.

Still off guard, Sam was immobile at first. "Yeah, sure," he said. He got up, reaching in his pocket for money. But Bill had already laid a couple of twenties on the table. Sam's eyes went from Bill to the money and back. Bill smiled slyly out one corner of his mouth and turned toward the door.

Sam hurried after him, regretting somewhat this turn of the conversation, but something inside him, his fantasies or some obsession not quite clear to him, pushed him on. His hands were shaking as he caught the door behind Bill and followed him out. He was acutely aware that his stomach was still empty; even the two drinks he'd had were making his head swirl. Hesitantly, he said, "I've got to get something to eat."

Swaying slightly, Bill said, "That's a good idea."

Watching Bill for an "okay," Sam stepped past him. Bill followed toward the small Chinese cafe on the corner.

After they were seated, Bill rolled his head back slightly and confided, "I'm getting drunk."

"You going to be okay?"

"I'm not going to be sick or anything."

On impulse, Sam said, "Let's go to my place. It's just a couple of blocks. We'll take the food with us. You can relax there."

Again pausing, Bill replied, "All right. That would be good." He breathed what seemed a sigh of relief.

As Sam ushered Bill into his living area, Bill pulled off his coat and dropped it on the floor next to the dowdy brown stuffed chair, sitting down. Sam was relieved. No shoulder holster, no gun, no sign of a weapon at all. What did you expect? he thought tensely.

They ate and Bill grew more comfortable. And quieter. Sam was feeling better with something in his stomach, too. He moved to get the conversation going again.

"Another drink?" he coaxed.

"Whattaya got?"

"No vodka. Sorry. I have some beer, a little white wine and some bourbon."

"Bring on the bourbon."

Sam poured a tall glass for Bill, a small wine for himself.

"What a week, huh?" he said, sipping the wine. Bill had already downed half his glass.

"Yeah. Looks like it's going to be spring finally." He was silent again, staring somewhere past his glass but not quite as far as where Sam sat. Sam watched him finish the drink and got up and poured another.

"Thanks," Bill muttered.

"You okay, Bill? You seem worried about something. Anything I can do? Is it your mother?"

"Yes, no. Just a lot of things. It's okay. Don't worry," he waved his hand in dismissal.

"Anything I can help with?" Sam attempted. "Sometimes it helps to talk."

Bill's look seemed to be one of longing, as though he'd had no one to talk to for a long time. Sam was unsure. He felt scared. His eyes locked into Bill's, he rose on shaky legs and walked toward him.

"You look really beat," he said and laid a hand on Bill's shoulder. Bill stiffened, then relaxed. Sam placed his other hand on Bill's back, his blood pounding. Without turning, Bill raised his right hand and placed it over Sam's. Something was definitely happening. Sam grinned to himself as his fear began to ease.

CHAPTER FOUR

Sam felt a swirl of confusion. He liked Bill, but it reminded him a little of times with his wife. Ex-wife, he reminded himself with a surge of anger. She had reeled him in with her little oh-so-sincere tricks, and he'd learned them well. Now, he was again focused. He wanted to find out about Bill. What he was really up to. His eyes narrowed as he leaned forward and patted Bill's hand. Bill turned slightly, giving Sam's hand a quick squeeze.

"You need another drink," said Sam, smiling as he tapped Bill on the cheek. Retreating to the kitchen, Sam clenched his jaws.

When he returned, Bill had unbuttoned the top buttons of his shirt and was looking very relaxed. Once again, Sam remembered his ex-wife, how she teased him. He set down Bill's bourbon and seated himself across from him.

"I'm glad we got together," he told Bill. He said it coyly, but his heart pounded with nervousness and anger.

Bill looked up at him, a little surprised. "I," he began. "Me, too, Sam," he said softly.

Cutting his eyes to the floor, Sam said as shyly as he could, "It's been a long time. I ..." The stammer was involuntary as he tried to control himself. "Not since my wife. Well, I don't mean." He stopped with purposeful silence.

"It's okay," Bill nodded. After a moment of gazing out the window, he continued, "I had this girlfriend. Well, like a wife, I guess." His eyes met Sam's.

Sam swallowed and drew his lips tight. "Yeah," he replied in understanding.

"Anyway, it just went wrong after a couple of years. Who the hell knows."

Sam saw his chance. He hoped. "Women," he said scornfully.

Bill shook his head slowly and stared at the floor again. "No shit."

Sam went to the kitchen and brought the bourbon to fill Bill's glass. He was charged with excitement, feeling he was on a roll. "Remember when you were a kid?"

Bill cocked his head questioningly. Sam couldn't help but smile. The gesture was kind of cute. "When I was a kid," he went on, "I used to see all these movies. And TV shows. You know, adventures, mysteries?" Fixing Bill with his gaze, he said, "I loved the ones where the guy was a hitman. Those guys were so exhilarating." He carefully poured bourbon over the swallow of wine left in his glass and downed it quickly. With a slow smile, he searched Bill's eyes.

"Yeah?" Bill said. He seemed unsure of his words.

"Ye-ah." Sam drew out the word slowly.

Silence filled the room.

"Sam," Bill said with a pained expression.

"Bill," Sam rushed. "It's good to get to know you." Then he didn't know what else to say.

Bill dropped his eyes to the floor, and with a great sigh, looked back at Sam. "You, too."

I've got him, Sam told himself. He rose and crossed to Bill and filled Bill's glass, even though Bill had barely touched the drink. Then he filled his own glass and ambled through the apartment shutting off lights. All except the lamp across from Bill and the one next to the bed. Again he sat opposite Bill.

"It's been quite a day for you. You want to stretch out?"

"Hmm?" Bill said, his glass teetering near his lips.

"Go to bed. I mean, maybe you'd like to get some sleep."

"Uh, yeah. I guess I ought to go."

"Hey, no, Bill. You don't have to worry about that. It's okay. Just relax. Use the bed if you want."

Bill looked with droopy eyelids. "I'll just finish this." He eased the glass up and sipped.

"Take your time." Sam leaned back on the couch, allowing his head to tilt back as he closed his eyes and let out a deep sigh. It was suddenly very quiet.

After several minutes, Sam peered through barely parted eyelashes. Bill sat in the same position, his chin beginning to bob toward his chest. Sam waited, then silently rose and crossed to Bill. He took the glass; Bill stirred only slightly as he relaxed his grip and let his arm drop. He looked out of it, all right. Sam returned to the couch.

Sam awoke bewildered. Bill's snore was just audible; it must have been what woke him. Sam looked at his watch: 2:15.

Bill's head was back against the cushion, his arms dropped to his sides in the chair. He looked very vulnerable. But was he?

Slowly, Sam crept to Bill's side. There was still no movement. "Bill," he whispered.

Bill's eyebrows rose slightly, but otherwise he did not move.

Sam's thumping heart rose up to his throat and he swallowed hard to calm his nerves.

"Joey," he said quietly.

"Mmm." Bill looked like he was trying to open his eyes. Sam cautioned himself to be careful.

"Joey wants to know."

Again Bill muttered, something sounding remotely like "What?"

"That you, Will?" Sam said in a raspy whisper.

"Who?" barely escaped Bill's lips as his eyes rolled beneath heavy lids.

"It's Joey. Joey wants to know if Barry found you."

"Bah, Barry," Bill snarled.

Sam was biting his lip. "Thursday, April 20th. What time?"

"Mmm-what?" One eye barely opened then shut. Sam ducked out of sight. After a long moment he whispered, "Do you remember the time?"

"Eleven-thirty, you snake." This time his head wobbled and his arms began to move slightly. Sam gulped and let the minutes pass. He walked behind Bill's chair and gently touched his hair. It was slightly damp with perspiration. Lightly he stroked along Bill's temple.

"Shh," he said. "It's okay." Then as he eased the tips of his fingers along Bill's neck, he just breathed, "Carlo's."

Bill nodded ever so slightly. "Carlo's."

The moment was here. Sam's hands were shaking so much he pulled them away from Bill. "Who, Will?"

"Hmm?"

"Who's the target?"

Bill was quiet. Sam was afraid he had missed the chance.

But then Bill mumbled, "Lastretto."

Sam's mouth dropped open. "Who?"

"Sss ... Sal Lastretto."

Wide-eyed, Sam stepped back, almost tipping the glass and quickly steadying it. Sal Lastretto. He'd read the name in the paper last week. One of the mob old-timers, and the feds were trying to indict him on something. Sam couldn't recall what.

Sam couldn't believe it. Still shaking, he slipped back to the couch where he sat watching Bill. Beginning to get his wits, he reached over and switched off the lamp. Only the glow from the bedroom, and the city lights through the window, lit the room. His stomach was so nervous, he felt sick.

Sal Lastretto. April 20.

Chapter Five

It was almost dawn, a faint glow seeping through the window. Sam sat gnawing the knuckle of his left thumb, unable to sleep or relax. Stealing the details out of Bill had been even scarier than overhearing the rest of it on the stairs. And more exciting.

For hours he had turned the information over and over in his mind, trying to figure what to do. Sam remembered the picture of Sal Lastretto in the paper. That smug bastard, all dapper and grinning. He reminded Sam of his father, always dressed up in his suit and tie, ready to run off on another business trip. He was a consulting representative with a large aeronautics company that had big government contracts around the country and around the world. He was always ready to roll over for his government handlers. Wasn't he just like Lastretto?

Sam wanted in. In on the deal. The hit, not the money. Although all that money certainly had its appeal.

Could he approach Bill about it? No. It was ridiculous. A professional assassin was not likely to discuss the affair with him. But what about what he had already learned? Why would Bill tell him all this?

Because Bill was only confirming what he thought someone else already knew. He was too drunk to realize it was Sam doing the asking.

Right now Sam just wanted to get rid of Bill so he could think. But he couldn't really do that. He needed to maintain a connection with Bill, get closer to him. He needed to bleed all the information possible from him.

Bill began to stir, and Sam straightened his knees and quietly stretched out on the couch. He pretended to be asleep, passed out. From under his arm he could see Bill blinking and looking around in confusion. Then, apparently realizing where he was, he touched his right hand to his forehead with a grimace. Sam remained still as Bill rose and uncertainly approached him. With sleepy eyes he looked up at Bill.

"Sorry, man," Bill said. "I guess I passed out."

"Ohhh. Me, too."

"I gotta go."

Making no effort to get up, Sam said, "Oh. You want some breakfast or something?"

With his hand to his stomach, Bill replied, "Ah, no thanks. I just need ..."

Sam pointed toward the bathroom.

Bill must have been about to burst from the sound of things. He hadn't closed the bathroom door and Sam eased up to peek over the arm of the couch.

He lay back down as Bill finished, then nonchalantly opened his eyes when Bill returned to the room.

"I gotta go," Bill repeated.

"Mmm, okay," Sam faked. "Maybe give me a call."

"Sure. See you."

"See you at work," Sam called as the door closed.

Bill was gone.

Sam immediately had his feet on the floor. He waited to

make sure Bill wouldn't return, then hurried to the window and looked down to the street. Bill was just coming out of the building, looking first one way and then the other before hurrying east.

For some time Sam stared at the quiet street below, then he slowly backed away to the center of the room. He was almost overwhelmed as the events of the evening cascaded in on him.

"Jesus," he said.

He raced into the bathroom and turned on the shower and started shedding his clothes. As he stood waiting for the water to adjust, he noticed the toilet, still open from when Bill had used it. With a chill he turned to view himself in the mirror. For a moment his lower lip quivered and then he jumped into the shower.

Dressed in jogging shoes, shorts and a T-shirt, Sam ran west toward the Hudson River. He needed to unwind, to think through what he'd got himself into. It was still early, only about 7, as he started south along the river.

Events flashed through his mind, the scene on the stairs, his discussion with Bill in the bar, the evening at his apartment. He had already run a couple of miles and was approaching the park near the World Financial Center before he slowed to a lope and began walking. After he passed Stuyvesant High School and entered the park, Sam found a bench facing Hoboken across the river. The early morning air was chilly against his glistening skin. Sam knew he should have brought a sweatshirt or towel. Nevertheless he sat there, his panting slowing, enjoying the stimulating breeze. A lone tug worked its way down the Hudson with its barge in tow. The sun glittering off the buildings over in New Jersey and reflecting off the river had an almost hypnotic effect. Sam shook his head and sat upright.

"I could do this," he whispered. "And he can't stop me."

Sam realized there was a lot of work to do. He had thought, no, fantasized, about this for years. He clenched his jaw remembering when he was 13 and his father had gone to consult with the Saudis and just didn't come back. Not that Sam missed him. His parents did nothing but argue when his father was around. His father was so full of advice about how his mother should raise Sam, but then he'd just go off "for his government" again. Good riddance.

And now Sam faced the opportunity to deal with Lastretto, another know-it-all.

With a wave of clarity, Sam knew he was ill-prepared. The library; no, gun shops. No, both. But he would have to be very careful. God! So little time, 11 days. And so much to do.

Sam jogged back to his apartment and hopped into the shower to soak up steam and gather his thoughts. And make a mental list.

Okay, he hadn't shot a gun since ROTC, 12 or 13 years ago. His mother had freaked, but he had been pretty good at it. In fact, the sergeant had told Sam he'd make a good sniper. And the feel ... it was thrilling. But that was an M16, not an Uzi, not a shotgun. And not a 10mm automatic pistol. He knew he could do it, but still.

First things first, he decided. Quickly, he dressed and hurried to the main public library on Fifth Avenue where the only magazines he found were for hunters. He pulled the newest books on the subject that looked like they might help, but no good. New York was really becoming a bunch of weenies in this area. He needed better info.

Over on 42nd Street he browsed through the news stores. This was better. He found what he was looking for.

The distractions around Times Square tempted him to blow it all off. But no. He had work to do.

Gun stores. In Manhattan? Should he go to Brooklyn? No doubt there were some great places to buy something there, but not legally. Better if he went to Long Island. Or Connecticut, home of Colt. Or Ohio or someplace. Well, he'd know more when he had gone through the magazines.

Back at his apartment, Sam began poring through them. It was a different world; these magazines were more extreme than the one he'd been reading at his desk at work. Minutes passed. Hours. He was beginning to visualize himself handling the weapons, formulating a plan for April 20.

He replayed the scene on the stairs again and again, and then the part where he extracted the final bit of information from Bill. It was easier than he'd dreamed, and had moved much faster than he had expected.

Ring!

The telephone jolted him from his fantasy.

Ring!

Damn. Who could it be? Probably his mother. That's all he needed.

But he could ignore her. No, she'd just get suspicious. She always did. He would have to answer.

"Hello," he said in a monotone.

"Sam? It's Bill. You there?"

Sam hadn't expected this. "Uh, yeah. I'm, I'm here."

"You okay, man? Or are you hung over like me?" Bill chuckled.

"Yeah, I guess I am." Sam's mind whirled for a response that made sense.

"I thought you might like to catch some dinner. This afternoon. If you're up for it," Bill said. After a brief pause with no response, he added, "We could make it an early evening so we don't have a repeat of last night."

Finally, Sam's brain kicked in. "No, I mean, yeah, that sounds good. And don't worry about last night. I'm feeling pretty good now. How about you?"

Bill laughed. "It was touch-and-go for a while there. I'm not sure how I even got home."

"You cut out of here like a rocket," Sam said without thinking.

"Habit, I guess."

"Quick exits before the old man returns, hey?" Sam responded quickly.

"Hah. Anyway, how about dinner?"

"Sure. Sounds good. Want to meet somewhere?"

"Why don't I meet you at your place?"

"Right," Sam said, wondering.

"Seven o'clock? Six?"

Sam looked at his watch: 4:30. It was later than he thought. "Let's make it 7," he said hesitantly.

"Want it later?" Bill asked.

"No, 7 is fine. You remember how to get here?" Sam grinned to himself, remembering Bill's condition last night.

"No problem. I could find it drunk."

Two and a half hours. Sam hadn't eaten all day, but he was

determined to spend the next couple of hours reading through the magazines and then he'd hit the shower again.

Sam tapped his nails on the kitchen table, trying to quell a feeling of panic. Was he ready for this?

Why not? he admonished himself. Get closer to the guy. Use him.

He began to formulate questions to work into the dinner conversation as he flipped through the magazines. Obviously, Bill knew a lot that would help Sam. He was the professional, after all. There must be a way to get him to talk.

Sam paced the apartment, imagining himself at the restaurant where Lastretto was having lunch. There was a guard standing near Lastretto. Maybe another covering the door. Sam would have to be just another customer.

He smiled, remembering the plays he'd acted in when he was in high school and college and the little theater group in Queens where he'd met his wife. She'd been so bright and energetic, so eager to play opposite Sam's lead role. They'd dated and things clicked.

Sam ruefully shook his head. He'd been so dumb.

When he'd been angry at his father for leaving them, Sam's mother was always telling him he was a good man, not like his father, but sweet and decent.

And innocent. After he'd married Deb and helped her get the female lead in the play, things between them began to cool off fast.

He had to laugh at himself. "The play's the thing," he chuckled bitterly. It was always mesmerizing to enter those "other worlds" of the characters he'd played.

Purposefully, still half grinning, Sam strode to the closet and extracted a large garment box. After the slightest hesitation, he set it on the bed and opened it. There was his collection of professional makeup plus the mustaches, eyebrows and wigs he'd acquired over the years. He unbuttoned his shirt and ran trembling fingers across his chest. He had to force himself to look at the clock.

5:52. There was just enough time, he assured himself, stripping off the rest of his clothes. There had to be!

Chapter Six

When Bill buzzed, Sam was sitting on the sofa, breathing deeply and exhaling slowly. Seven on the dot. No surprise.

"Come on down," said Bill. "I have a cab waiting."

Sam was caught off guard but answered smoothly, "Right." He was determined to be in control.

He emerged from his building dressed in dark tan slacks and a brown casual jacket. Bill stood by the taxi in an expensive gray suit with a dark green and blue designer tie.

"Oh, let me go change," Sam stammered. He cursed himself.

"Don't worry about it," Bill replied jovially, opening the taxi door.

"Well, I ..."

"You're fine. Come on."

Sam clenched his jaw and ducked into the cab.

"Okay," Bill said to the driver and the cab sped away.

"Where are we going?"

"Quiet little place, good food," Bill interrupted.

Sam did not feel the control he had intended.

There was a moment of silence, but Bill quickly followed with, "What have you been up to today?"

"Ah," Sam began. Then his mind slipped into gear. "Believe

it or not, I was up running by 7 and --"

"You, too?"

Sam was genuinely surprised. "You run in the morning?"

"Seems like I spend half my life running. To or from something." He grinned as his elbow slightly jabbed Sam's arm. Sam smiled too.

"Well, I mean, do you run in events?"

"No. I don't have time for that. I just like to stay in shape. Work out, run, karate. You never know." He jabbed the air quickly and Sam instinctively jerked his right arm up in a block.

"Hey, pretty good," Bill said. "We should go a couple of rounds."

"I'm afraid I don't know any karate." Sam chose not to mention the training he'd had for one of the plays he was in a couple of years back.

"Could have fooled me," Bill chuckled.

Good, thought Sam.

"Right around the corner on 95th," Bill directed the driver. "Pull up right there."

The old stone building had a small gracefully lettered sign: Eddie's Cuisine. Sam looked up and down the quiet tree-lined street. A classy block, expensive cars. But Bill was already opening the door to the restaurant.

Before Sam could reach the threshold, a deeply tanned man with perfectly cut gray hair and an immaculate dark blue suit grasped Bill by the shoulders.

"Will! It's been too long!"

"Eddie. How have you been? This is Sam," Bill said, extending his arm toward Sam.

"Good to meet you, Sam." With a beautiful, broad smile,

Eddie shook Sam's hand. "Come on in, gentlemen. I'll have a table ready in a few minutes." As he ushered them through the door, he raised his hand and snapped his fingers. There was nothing said, but two waiters hurried toward the tables.

Sam scanned the room. There were about 20 tables, and they all looked taken. But the waiters descended on what appeared to be the lone unoccupied spot in the back corner, away from the bar and at the opposite end of the wall from the kitchen entrance.

Eddie led Sam and Bill to the bar.

"Anthony, bring the best champagne." As the barman poured, Eddie handed the first glass to Bill.

"It's the closest we have to the fatted calf," he said, looking into Bill's eyes. "Welcome home, Will."

Bill nodded with a shy smile. "Eddie's quite a guy," he said raising his glass. "Come on, Sam." He tipped the glass toward Eddie and drank the champagne. Sam followed suit, curious about the ceremony.

The barman refilled the glasses. Eddie said, "Gentlemen, your table is ready," and a waiter led them to it.

"What was all that?" Sam asked after they were seated.

"Eddie and I go way back," Bill replied, not really looking at Sam. "It's been a long time since I was here."

His tone became lighter. "The food is wonderful," he said, handing Sam a menu. "Take a look. But if you have no objection, we can just let Eddie decide. We can't go wrong."

Sam held the menu half open for a moment, then closed it. "Sounds good to me. Bring on the feast."

Course after course, Sam studied Bill. He was at ease, almost a different person. In fact, Sam would say he had completely dropped his guard. Perhaps he would now be more open. Sam knew he shouldn't let the chance pass.

He kept his conversation simple, letting Bill do most of the talking. Bill praised the veal piccata and the restaurant, and chatted with the staff. Finally, after a wonderful tiramisu, they were settling with glasses of sambuca. Sam said, "This is really nice, Bill. Like an adventure."

"Yeah, Eddie really knows how to lay down a meal."

"So different from what I usually do," Sam said. "Say, do you like to hunt?" he asked abruptly.

"What?" said Bill with an uncertain half grin.

"I mean, take guns and things. I always liked guns and hunting." Reaching and touching Bill's arm, he hurried on. "Wouldn't it be great to go on one of those African safaris? Or maybe wild boar down in Mexico or somewhere?"

Bill seemed unsure, wrinkling up his nose. "Nah, I don't go for guns much."

"Really?" Sam responded with more surprise than he'd wished. "I mean, you seem like the sort."

"What sort?"

"Well," he struggled to regain control, "adventurous."

"I like to think I am adventurous."

Sam had mixed feelings about Bill's inviting smile. There was too much at stake to weaken now. "Yeah, there's more than one kind of adventure, that's for sure."

Again he touched Bill's arm, just a light brush this time. "This is all so fine," he said softly. "But I tell you, this cowboy's about run out of steam."

Bill cocked his head in that same cute boyish way as last night. Sam could see this was not what Bill had expected.

"I'm going to have to head for home."

"Hey, we're just getting started here," Bill protested.

"I guess last night is catching up with me. And I've got to get out and see my mother," he quickly added.

Bill straightened a little. "Ah, yes. That is important."

At Sam's slight shrug, Bill said, "Hey, no problem. We've had a nice evening, and all good things have to end sometime."

Sam nodded, smiling, and reached for his wallet.

"No way," said Bill. "This is my treat."

But suddenly, Eddie was standing there. "You're both wrong, gentlemen. This is the pleasure of the house."

"Now, Eddie," began Bill.

"I insist." Then that winning smile again. "But you must come back soon."

They got up and Bill was shaking Eddie's hand. Sam saw him stuff a $100 bill into Eddie's pocket. "See that the waiters get a little of that," he smiled.

"They will enjoy it all."

As they walked toward Broadway to hail a cab, Sam said, "Sorry to spoil the evening, man."

Bill stopped and looked at him. "You didn't spoil the evening. You *were* the evening."

Again Sam felt like he and Bill were old friends. It was difficult to maintain his resolve. But he must.

Bill offered to take him home, but Sam declined. "I know you live up here," he said. "We'll talk later."

As they shook hands, he held Bill's hand a moment and then got in the cab and closed the door. Bill watched him drive away.

CHAPTER SEVEN

S am had already run and showered and was on the train munching a bagel by 8:30 Sunday morning. That he was going to his mother's on Long Island was true, but that was hardly his real destination. He had kept his mother's house as his address even though he'd lived in Manhattan for two years; it avoided a lot of hassles and allowed him a place to keep his '85 Camaro.

At the train station in Copiague, Sam took a taxi. Though his mother knew he was coming, he didn't want to "owe" her for the ride. He had breakfast with her (there was no way he could avoid that), but declined church. And as he'd expected, he had to insist that she go ahead without him. He wanted to drive around a little, he told her.

With his mother finally on her way, Sam set out for Farmingdale to visit a couple of the biggest gun stores on Long Island.

"I'm looking for something in the way of self-defense," Sam told the clerk who wore a not-so-concealed holster holding a small automatic stuffed in the top of his pants.

"You do much shooting?"

"Not for a while."

Starting to the other end of the long counter, the man said, "It's up to you to decide whether you want an auto or a revolver, but I'd recommend starting with this 357 Magnum. Easy to handle, packs plenty of power. Some of the bigger ones buck pretty hard when you're not used to it."

Sam reached out to take the shiny pistol.

"You got your license, right?" said the man, hesitating.

"What do you mean?"

"Handgun license."

"Well, no, not yet."

"Sorry. I can't even let you handle it if you don't have a license."

"You're kidding."

"You got your application in?" the clerk asked.

"I, uh, guess I'm going to have to do that. How long does it take?"

"Four or five months. Just be glad you don't live in the city. It's almost impossible to get one there."

Great, thought Sam, shaking his head in frustration. "Okay," he said, "let's say I get my application in for a handgun. But in the meantime ..."

"You'd still like to have something for home defense?"

"Right."

"I got just what you need," the man told him, and started back to where they'd first met. Sam tore his eyes from the big automatics in the showcase and followed.

"The problem with a lot of handguns is they're too dangerous anyway," the clerk was telling him. He could see he had Sam's attention. ".38, 9mm and bigger, bullet could go right through your walls and into a neighbor's. Now this," he said, hoisting up a short-barreled shotgun with a pistol grip, "is another story." Operating the pump action with a commanding metallic click-clack, he handed the gun to Sam. "Intruder in your home is going to recognize that sound immediately."

Sam held the shotgun, admiring its light weight. But it just didn't fit the image he'd had, the "glamour" of the big automatic. His mind raced. April 20. He had to figure something.

"But what about maneuverability?" he asked. "You hear somebody in the house and you're going down the hallway --"

"That's the nice thing about this baby. With the pistol grip and no stock, it's easy to handle, to swing around in that hallway, if you need to. And," he confided, "when you pull the trigger, you'll hit anything in the room. That's where you have a real advantage over a handgun, especially in the dark. And your shot is going to go into the walls. And the bad guy. Not into your neighbor's kid three houses away."

As Sam lifted the shotgun, he noted the ease of operating the pump as he pondered the words, "hit anything in the room." This wasn't right, not what he had been fantasizing about. But ...

"You can walk out with that today."

Sam had spied what looked like assault rifles. "What about these?"

"Oh, those ... they give guns a bad name. You know, all that press and all."

"Wouldn't they work pretty good as self-defense?"

"Same problem as handguns, except worse. High velocity, multiple rounds before you can stop to think."

"But you have them for sale," Sam observed.

"They're more for collectors. I mean, they're not exactly hunting rifles. And, price -- $900 for this AK-47. And that shotgun you're holding ..."

"Yeah?" prompted Sam.

"$288."

Sam chewed at the inside of his cheek. "I see what you mean," he said. He knew he had to make a decision. He just wasn't ready.

Reluctantly, he handed the shotgun back to the man. "I appreciate your information," he said. "I'll need to think about it."

The man smiled as Sam turned to leave. "They'll tell you the same at Edelman's. And we can beat their price."

Sam nodded with a grin. "Okay. How late you open?"

"We'll be here till 5." ·

The man was right. On Sam's next shopping round, the clerk immediately steered him to the same style shotgun. And since Sam already knew the score with handguns, he didn't press it (except to look longingly at them before leaving). In the end, though, he'd made up his mind.

This store had an even better selection of new and used assault-style rifles. Although a couple weren't much longer than the long-barreled .50 Magnum automatic pistol.

"How about these?" he asked the clerk. "I've been reading about some of them."

The clerk, older than the one he'd talked to at the first store, eyed him a minute. "Look," he said, dropping the salesman's edge a little, "if you're really interested in something like this, you can't beat this AK-47 here." He handed it over to Sam and watched with what looked like a tinge of pride. This information pretty much agreed with what Sam had read.

Sam ran his hand down the front stock, turning the gun

over slowly. He realized the salesman was studying him.

"You have a personal interest in this one?" he asked.

"Well, no," the man replied, clearly caught off guard. Then, "Yeah. Belongs to a friend of mine. His wife hates the thing," he said, leaning across the counter toward Sam. "I think she's jealous."

Sam smiled knowingly.

"And he can use the money."

Sam looked at the price tag and purposefully scowled and screwed up his lips. "$825?" he asked, unbelieving. "I'll give you $700."

"Seven and a quarter," the man quickly replied.

Sam nodded. "Done."

Twenty minutes later, after haggling again when the $50 sales tax was being added, Sam walked out with the gun, two boxes of ammo and a much lighter Visa card.

He drove around awhile to calm down from the excitement. And stopped for a slice of pizza and an Orangina. He didn't want to appear too eager by going back to the first store so soon, so he pulled into a shopping center to browse some books. And there was the big Kmart sporting goods store.

"What the hell," he mused. "Might as well save a few more bucks."

This time, when he got to the guns section, he went right to the clerk, a young man who appeared to be no more than 18, and said, "I want to look at the Remington 12-gauge."

"Sure," the young man said, turning toward the rack of shotguns.

"No," said Sam. "The short-barreled defense gun with the pistol grip."

"Right." The clerk scurried over and handed him the gun.

"How much?" Sam asked him.

Pulling up the tag, the clerk said, "$255."

Sam lingered, carefully sighting down the barrel and operating the pump action. He laid the gun on the counter. "Fine. I'll take it."

This time he got three boxes of shells.

Sam could feel his mother watching him over the fragrant pot roast she had prepared for dinner. He had tried not to let it show how preoccupied he was, but she always knew.

"Something's troubling you, Samuel."

Sam grasped onto something. "It's the ... too much work. I need to get away for a while."

"Away?"

"Oh, just away from the city."

"You're always welcome here, dear."

"Oh, I know. I appreciate that, Mom." Sam tried to make his smile warm instead of sardonic. "You have Uncle Jack's number?" he added casually.

"Uncle Jack? You mean your father's sister?" She always called him "your father."

"Her ex-husband, Mom."

"Yes, of course. I know what you mean," she said stiffly. "Why do you want their number?"

"I was thinking of going up there. Take a long weekend, cruise around the Finger Lakes and go on down to Elmira to their farm."

"Samuel, when was the last time you saw them?" she asked. She sounded suspicious.

"What difference? He always liked me."

"And you liked him?" She raised an eyebrow.

"Sure. He's a nice man. Salt of the earth and all that."

"What are you up to?"

"I told you. I just want to get away to the country. Do you have their number?" Sam was getting impatient.

"Yes, of course. I can get it right now."

"Mom," he said, staying her arm as she started to rise, "I'm sorry. After dinner's fine. Let's eat, okay? This is good."

As he drove away from the trim little white house, Sam had a rush of childhood memories. His mother had been so sweet then. But after Sam's father left, she became more rigid. She seemed afraid, unsure, insecure. But relieved.

The money still came from Sam's father for a while and Sam's mom took the reins. She made sure the nice home in Port Washington was paid for and bought a small house in Lindenhurst which she rented out for income. When Sam started college, she sold the larger home and moved to the little one. She helped Sam with expenses through college and was always there when he was troubled.

How does she always know? Sam wondered. Of course he'd been too outwardly nervous this evening, but how could he not?

Anyway, this part was done. It would be a pain to keep his car in the city, but it was better than coming back here to pick it up. At least he'd planned that out.

Sam made the drive back to Manhattan in the heavy Sunday evening traffic and pulled into a small parking lot on West Street. He called his uncle that night.

"Uncle Jack? It's Sam Robbins ... Yes, that's right, Ben's boy."

His uncle was his regular country self. It amazed Sam sometimes how far apart New York City was from the rest of the state.

"I'm going to be up in your area next weekend and thought I'd stop in and see you and Linda." She was never Aunt Linda, but for some reason, her husband was always Uncle Jack.

It only took a few minutes and everything was arranged. Even if they weren't home when he got there, Sam knew he could browse around the farm. And find a good place to do some target practice.

CHAPTER EIGHT

Monday was quite another thing. Sam wanted to get as close to Bill as possible in order to find out all he could and solidify his plans. He even had in mind to follow Bill. But he was finding the relationship a drain.

Sam kept up a very brisk pace on the way to work. The morning went by quickly enough, but his stomach began to get jittery as lunchtime neared. He wanted to go out and walk, to get away. Did he really have to try to see Bill?

At 11:30 Sam wandered down to the cafeteria, hoping to peek in quickly, confirm that Bill was not there and leave for his walk. When he got there, though, he decided to go ahead and get a sandwich. He would walk it off.

He was beginning to feel relieved as he paid and headed to the windows in the back.

"Hey, Sam," came a voice from behind him. Bill was in one of the small "booths" set off by temporary dividers. He beckoned for Sam to sit.

Sam hesitated only a moment and then turned on his smile. "How you been?"

"How'd it go?" Bill was already asking.

"Huh?"

"Your mother. How was the visit?"

"Oh," Sam slowly nodded. "It was fine. You know, a little

hassle here, a little hassle there," he laughed.

"Yeah," said Bill. "How's her health? Okay?"

"Oh," Sam almost snorted, "she's healthy as a horse. I should be so lucky if she wasn't."

At Bill's frown, Sam added, "Just a joke. A bad joke."

"Right."

Sam watched as Bill flipped his index finger back and forth over the corner of the paper napkin on his tray. He waited, somewhat annoyed at this childish display.

"Sam," Bill finally said.

"Yeah?" said Sam as if totally unconcerned.

Bill frowned down at his plate. "I was wondering ..."

Sam paused, worried that something had happened. He regretted his callous response a moment ago. "What is it?"

"I've got some tickets to this play tomorrow night." He studied Sam carefully. "I wonder if you would like to go."

Sam stopped in midbite. He couldn't believe this shyness from Bill. But he knew he'd better "fix" what he'd likely almost damaged. "Tomorrow?" he said. "Hey, that sounds great."

There was an almost audible sigh from Bill. And a slight smile.

Sam moved ahead. "Maybe we could get together after work and talk about it."

Again that worried look in Bill's eyes.

"It'll give me this afternoon to make a couple of calls and make sure everything's clear Tuesday."

"Of course," Bill smiled.

"After work, then? 4:30?" Sam asked.

"Sure."

"I've got to get on back to my desk," Sam apologized. "We

got these problems," he scowled. Then he grinned.

"After work," Bill agreed.

Sam knew he had to control his impatience. He did not look forward to a whole evening wasted, but maybe this would give him a chance to find out more.

Bill was waiting in the lobby after work and they went to the same bar they'd stopped at on Friday.

"All right," said Sam, "you're on. What's the play?"

"A little production I read about. I think you'll like it. If you don't have plans, you want to get some dinner?" After starting out with the calm and control that Sam had initially characterized as Bill, Bill was faltering again.

"Sure," Sam said. "My treat this time?" He pondered where to go.

"That's not necessary. You did get dinner on Friday."

"Chinese takeout hardly compares with Chez Eddie," Sam chuckled. This seemed to put Bill at ease again.

"Okay, we'll work that out. Hey, I know this Mexican place up on Third. Interested?"

"You know a lot of places," Sam kidded. "Lead on."

Though it was a mild evening, Bill hailed a cab when they were on the street and in 20 minutes they arrived at a bright pink and dark green place near 50th called Cafe Felix.

It was another great meal, although the prices were what Sam could call affordable. And Bill didn't seem to have any intimate ties to the place.

After dinner, Bill ordered shots of silver tequila. "I promise not to overdo it like last Friday," he said, raising his glass in a short salute. "Why don't you come over to my place and I'll open a fresh bottle? Repay your hospitality," he added almost as a question.

Sam hadn't expected an invitation, but he didn't want to make the wrong move. With only the briefest pause, he raised his own glass with a sly smile. "To a fresh bottle."

Bill's place on West 83rd was a far cry from Sam's. After they stepped into the foyer, Sam wondered which apartment was Bill's. But Bill simply draped his coat on the stairs and Sam followed him into a well-furnished living room with a tan leather couch, an overstuffed recliner and a wall of shelves incorporating bookcases, TV and sound equipment. An oriental rug covered the hardwood floor between the couch and the shelves.

Sam's eyes darted about. "Uh, all this yours?"

Bill looked pleased.

Sam was amazed. To his right through a wide doorway was a dining room; beyond that was the kitchen, he guessed. The dining room was easily 10 x 12 with a six-foot oak table at one end surrounded by six matching chairs. Across from the table another fine-loomed rug lay before a glass-front china hutch. And on the other wall was an oak cabinet about 4 feet wide supporting a large flat screen. Two gold candlestick holders were to the right of the TV, the dining room and kitchen separated by a bar-height counter with a brass rail on the dining room side. Bill opened one of the cabinets above the rail and took out a bottle.

The bottle was clear but intricately carved, like fine crystal. On the front was a white label with gold and light green trim with words in Spanish.

"Got this when I was in Mexico," Bill smiled at him. "I

don't think you can find it here. It would probably cost too much if you could."

"How much did it cost there?" Sam made the stupid remark before he could stop himself.

But Bill didn't seem to notice. "It was a little over $50, I think."

"Dollars?" Sam stuttered. He did it again.

"Yes. You can buy just about anything for dollars there," Bill smiled smugly.

Snap went the seal on the bottle and Bill popped out the cork. He ceremoniously poured into a short-stemmed glass etched with frosted images of playful nymphs. "Try this," he said to Sam, and poured one for himself.

"Here's to a new beginning." Bill's eyes were bright and confident.

"New beginning?" Sam quizzed.

"New bottle." Bill was obviously amused with himself.

Sam took a sip. The liquor was smooth. So smooth. He drank another, larger, swallow. It was almost like air sliding over his tongue. Bill leaned with his back against the bar, sniffing at his glass with half-closed eyes and swaying his head.

Without warning, a glowing warmth began to spread through Sam. His ears felt flushed, his face numb and there was a tingling in his whole body.

"Whoa!" he said with a slow gasp.

Bill laughed. "I thought you might like it."

"Where did you -- man! This is tequila?"

"Ha, ha," Bill responded, and emptied his glass with one quick swig. "Bottoms up, Sam. We've got the whole bottle."

"Uh, Bill, I don't think I can drink the whole bottle."

Bill stared at him seriously for a second. "Good," he said, "because I'd hoped to have some of it, too."

Sam laughed this time and Bill joined him. Bill poured again.

In half an hour, the bottle sat half-empty on the counter as the two men lounged in the living room, Sam half-erect in the recliner and Bill facing him on the couch.

"I don't think I can dink another drop," Sam sighed.

"Dink?" asked Bill, amused.

"I mean, drink. You see?"

"I guess I do."

There was a moment's silence. Then Bill leaned forward. "Sam ..."

Sam's head was buzzing as he tried to maintain his focus. Finally, he was able to turn his face toward Bill. "What?"

Bill studied him. He spoke so softly Sam thought the buzzing in his head must be increasing. "You're a pretty good guy, Sam."

Bill was leaning closer and Sam blinked trying to figure out --

Bill's fingers lightly touched Sam's knee. "Would you like --"

Sam jerked in response. The glass in Bill's hand trembled near his lips. "Bill --"

"Sam --"

"Look, I ..."

As Sam struggled to get up from the chair, Bill stared up at him, his eyes like those of a scolded puppy. Slowly, he rose to face Sam, his breathing much more labored than that small effort could cause.

Sam could feel himself swaying and staggered to steady himself.

"Sam, you could stay here. We still have," he said, turning to look at the bottle on the counter, "a few more glasses to go."

Sam tried to see through the fog surrounding him. He was being seduced, that was clear. But he wasn't sure how he should respond. "Hey, man." He waved a hand haphazardly in Bill's direction. "I can't do this. I'm too messed up."

Again the hurt puppy frowned at him as Sam reached in to give his own brain a good shaking. The fog was beginning to clear some.

"It wouldn't be so good," he told Bill, "if I couldn't even remember anything."

Bill was staring at the floor. "Maybe it would be better forgotten."

"No." Sam gripped Bill's shoulder. "I just want to be here. You know?"

He studied Bill's face as Bill slowly raised his gaze. "I'm going to grab a cab. Try to make it home," Sam said quietly.

"I'll call you one."

Sam turned toward the hall, shaking his head with a weak smile. "I think I need the air."

"I'll walk with you, then."

"Sure."

Once again, Sam was sitting in a taxi as Bill stood on the curb watching him disappear. Sam's head swirled with intoxication, both physical and emotional. He'd need to be more in control next time.

CHAPTER NINE

When Sam returned from his morning stair climb, he had voicemail from Bill: Meet after work for the play? Are we still on?

The struggle in Sam's mind and heart had kept him tossing most of the night. He'd gotten maybe two hours of sleep. As soon as he heard Bill's voice on the message, his heart started beating like he'd run a dozen flights of stairs. What the hell was going on? he gasped to himself as he gripped the arm of his chair.

Bill seemed like a genuinely nice guy. A gentleman. Sam really liked him. And more. Even if he did know Bill was a ... Go ahead, he told himself. A killer.

And Sam wanted to enter the same line of work?

He was staring blankly at his empty desk shaking his head when he was startled by a voice.

"Hey, Sam." It was his supervisor. "Tough walk on the stairs? You're breathing kind of hard." The man wore his worst slimy lizard grin.

Sam wanted to jump up and choke him. Instead he clenched his jaw, inhaling deeply. The fog of last night and this morning was beginning to clear.

"You should try it sometime, Pee-ter. It might take some of the jounce out of your jowls."

Pete's head snapped back almost imperceptibly. "No need to get testy, old boy. Anyway," he added in his boring business manner, "I'm reminding you of the 4 o'clock meeting."

"Four!" Sam remarked before he could stop himself.

"We talked about this last week," Pete said stuffily. "It was on the email."

Again Sam managed to pause before replying. "Oh, yeah. I thought you meant the ..." He turned and flashed his best false smile, making no effort to hide his displeasure. "I'll be there with bells on."

"Never mind the bells," said the supervisor, turning on his heels. "Just be there."

With cold eyes Sam watched him leave. Thanks, Peter, he said to himself as a sneer spread over his face. Once again he was collected and focused. He knew he could do Bill's "job." He could make the hit.

Sam picked up the phone and punched in the number. "Hey, Bill. Slight change in plans." He relished the silence on Bill's end of the phone. "Got a meeting at 4, so I can't get away till after 5. Okay?"

"Oh. Sure," said Bill. He couldn't hide the hopeful relief in his voice. And Sam loved it.

"I hate to make you wait," Sam almost purred. "I'll call you when we're free. See you then." He smiled as he hung up.

Sam sailed through the rest of the day, hardly noticing the work as he made mental plans for his special day, Thursday, April 20.

Bill seemed a little edgy. Sam was afraid he'd overplayed it again. He would have to try to lighten things up.

"Those meetings are such a pain in the ass." Bill's half-smile made him feel a little better. Then Sam realized they were going away from the subway stop. "Hey, where are we going?"

"Oh, I thought we'd drive over," Bill said, almost as an afterthought.

"Drive uptown?"

"The play's in Brooklyn." He was handing over the ticket in the parking garage they had just entered.

"Brooklyn," Sam repeated.

As they both looked up the rampway, Sam pictured his old Camaro and wondered what would arrive for them. Bill stood quietly until a melodic hum flowed from the dimness of the ramp. He strode to the curb as a shiny black BMW M5 rolled to a halt and the valet held the door open. Bill slipped a bill into the man's hand; Sam couldn't tell how much.

"Well, come on," said Bill, half into the car.

Sam was still standing there like a gawking child. "Yeah," he said.

He settled into the rich smell of leather as Bill zipped into the traffic. Finally, Sam's brain was in control again. "Nice car," he said in an even voice.

"You like it?" Bill turned briefly toward him.

Like it? Is he crazy? thought Sam. But what he said was, "Sure. This one is definitely on my list."

Bill smiled broadly, his eyes returning to the maze of traffic.

Jeez. What is with him? wondered Sam. It's like he's on a date trying to impress his --

Sam glanced toward Bill, who seemed perfectly at ease as they headed toward the bridge. It was starting to drizzle but that in no way slowed Bill's progress. Bill was again relaxed. Confident.

A lump hardened in Sam's chest. Maybe Bill had figured him out. Maybe he was on his way right now to dump Sam in some --

"You're going to like this play," Bill said pleasantly without taking his eyes off the road.

Sam sighed the lump away. "Yeah? What's it about?"

"You'll see. A little surprise, huh?" He gave Sam a wicked smile. Sam began to worry more.

For a few minutes they cruised in silence. Sam noticed they had left the main streets and were heading into an area of large warehouses. There was very little traffic. In fact, Sam hadn't seen any people either.

It grew darker as the blocks became longer and longer, with streetlights only at the corners. The lump in Sam's chest felt huge.

"Uh, Bill, where are we?"

"What?" Bill seemed distracted.

Damn, thought Sam. I don't believe this. His voice quavered a little. "What is this area? What's, uh, what's going on?"

"Going on?" Bill just now noticed Sam's wide eyes. "What'd you think? I figured we'd get something to eat. The play doesn't start for a couple of hours."

Eat! Sam's brain echoed. A small gasp escaped before he could speak. "Oh, right." He had no idea where they were.

Suddenly, Bill downshifted two gears and whirled into an alleyway between two huge warehouses. Before Sam could think, they made another quick right and half-skidded to a halt next to a row of shiny, expensive cars. Past them was a large house with bright lights spraying onto the cars. Two older men in hats and perfectly tailored suits were escorted by a shapely young woman with a fur draped over one shoulder. Bill was already out of the car.

"Coming?" he said, leaning down to look over at Sam.

Quickly, Sam got out. As they approached the bright-lit door, he could hear laughter and loud conversation.

"Hey," said Bill, stopping suddenly. "I'm sorry. I didn't even ask. I hope this is all right. It's another place I know. Good food, nice atmosphere."

Sam was looking around, only half hearing Bill. "Oh," he said, much relieved. Then he fixed on Bill and smiled. "Sure," he shrugged. "This looks interesting."

Bill hesitated before returning the smile. "It certainly is that," he replied. "Come on. Let's go in."

The noise that hit them as they stepped through the etched-metal double doors reminded Sam of something out of an old cowboy movie when the hero walked into the saloon. There was laughter and loud talking. Smoke hung around the high ceilings where two fans worked to mix the mess. Only the music floating over the sounds of the people was different from the movie in his mind. It wasn't rinky-dink piano; Sam thought he recognized the soothing sounds of Sinatra.

The room itself was much like the warehouses they had passed, a very large area like a shop floor, set off by huge beam-like pillars near the corners. Beyond them the "center" of the room was edged by another 10 feet or so on each side where the ceilings were a normal 8 feet. These areas were darkened, with only a scattering of tables along the walls. Sam noticed that to the right of the entryway were stairs leading to a loft above the outer edges, with a railing all the way around. Were there more rooms up there? he wondered.

Most of the patrons were men, mostly in their 50s or older. They looked like successful businessmen, all in suits and ties, except that many had on hats and several wore dark glasses.

Bill nudged his arm. "You're staring, Sam. It will make people nervous."

Sam just said, "Uh," and followed Bill to a table near the back of the center-room.

A waiter hurried past, dropping menus for them. The sounds and smoke swirling around him, Sam half-whispered, "What is this place?"

Bill chuckled and leaned over nefariously. "Notorious hangout," he said, arching his eyebrows up and down.

Sam was sucked right in. "What do you mean? These guys look like the Mafia or something."

"Sam," Bill indulged, "a lot of them are." At Sam's silence, he added, "Don't make a deal. You don't want to upset them." Then he laughed and poked Sam on the shoulder.

"Come on, Sam. They have some great pasta here."

"Pasta," said Sam. It figured. "Sounds fine."

Bill laughed again and began browsing the large single-page menu.

Sam pretended to do the same, stealing glances around the room, and when Bill announced his preference, Sam said he would have that, too.

The place remained crowded, cigar and cigarette smoke heavy in the air. So much for smoking laws. People came and went, usually in groups of three or more, usually all men. There were only a few young women here and there. This obviously was not a place for wives.

Sam's cannelloni was delicious, as were the two glasses of Chianti. He was feeling relaxed when the bill came, but he realized he had seen no prices on the menu. Bill, who had had no wine to delay him, was already putting money down and seemed to be studying him.

"What?"

"We need to leave if we're going to get there in time. If you're finished, that is."

"Oh. Yeah," Sam nodded, pushing his wineglass aside.

Outside, Sam could still smell the tobacco. He felt like he needed a shower. But at least it was quiet. He could even hear the soft "whump" of the door closing. Bill watched him for a moment without saying a word, then backed the car around and whisked through the alley as though he had full knowledge that no other cars would be entering.

Finally, Sam said, "Quite a place."

"Yeah. You like it okay?"

Noting the lingering uncertainty in Bill's voice, Sam smiled. "Hey, it was an experience."

"Right," Bill laughed, "an experience."

The play was something else again. Sam hadn't known what to expect, but this lonely, haunting tale of two star-crossed lovers, both male, disturbed him. Why had Bill chosen this particular play? Was there a deeper message? And even without considering Bill's intentions, the play was plain depressing. Very well acted, but a real downer. Sam wanted to go home and get out of his smoky clothes and forget the whole story.

"How about a nightcap?" Bill asked as they drove away.

"I ... don't," Sam began. But he noticed Bill was the nervous teen again. "Sure. What did you have in mind?"

Bill's cautious smile thanked him. "You want to come by my place?" Sam's hesitation was obvious, but Bill was trying to show confidence, adding, "Or we could stop back by the place we had dinner."

Sam rolled his eyes in mock surrender. "Oh, no. Let's go to your place."

Bill was at ease again, pushing the M5 fluidly through traffic. He seemed to drive faster when he felt better.

As they sped along and Bill joked, Sam began to leave the drab nature of the play behind him. Then just as he was about to kid along with Bill, they were interrupted by bright flashing lights and the quick burp of a police siren.

"Pull over and turn off your engine," came the loud command broadcast from behind them.

Sam looked at Bill with concern, but Bill just shrugged and pulled to the curb.

Bill hit the button and the window slid silkily down as an officer approached. In the right mirror Sam could see another policeman getting out of the passenger side of the squad car.

"Step out of the car," said the officer, standing well back with his hand poised over his gun. A chill rushed through Sam. He was both excited and scared.

Carefully, Bill got out of the car, making sure his hands were in view of the cop. What next? wondered Sam.

"Hey," said the officer. Sam feared the worst. "Will? What the hell?"

"Mike," exclaimed Bill. "How you doing? You get a promotion?"

"Up yours, man," said Mike, slapping Bill playfully on the shoulder. "Hey, Earl," he called. "It's Will Peters."

Peters? wondered Sam.

"What's a snake like you doing with an M5," said Earl as he walked around the front of the squad car.

"Just lucky, I guess," Bill smiled.

"We clocked you at over 60 in a 30 zone back there," said Earl.

Bill grinned. "It's just hard to keep this sucker on the ground. You know?"

"No," Earl retorted icily, "I don't know."

"Well, why don't you guys drop around and take it for a ride sometime?"

"Yeah?"

"Here's my card," Bill said. "Give me a call. Real soon. It's a honey to drive."

"Damn!" said Mike, taking the card.

"Hey, Mike."

"Earl, he's serious."

"Come on, Earl," Bill said. "It won't bite you. It's just a car." Bill opened the door, and with a wink at Sam, grabbed something from the console compartment.

"Here you go, Earl," he said.

"What?"

"The keys, man. This way you guys can just pick it up at the garage after you call. And you can drive first." He dropped the keys in Earl's hand.

"Damn, Will!" said Mike, patting Bill on the shoulder.

Earl flashed a toothy grin. "Yeah. Uh, thanks, Will. That's, that's real nice of you."

Bill's voice was smooth and sincere. "What are friends for?"

Mike took Bill's hand. "Thanks, Will. Thanks a lot. You really mean it?"

"I really mean it."

There was silence all around, then Mike said, "Come on, Earl. Let's get going. The man's got places to go."

Earl held up the keys again and stared at them. "Right. Hey, thanks, Will. I'm sorry."

"Forget it, Earl," said Bill. "It's just like the old days, right? Buddies."

"See ya," Earl said, turning back to the police car.

"What was that all about?" Sam asked as Bill got in the car.

"A couple of old pals." Bill had started the engine and sped away from the curb.

"But," Sam stared anxiously toward the speedometer. "They nailed you for speeding."

"Like I said, a couple of old buddies." Sam thought he saw a twinkle in Bill's eye as Bill whipped the lever to third gear. He must have been going 60.

"Now about that nightcap."

"Bill," Sam's eyes pleaded as he glanced past the clock on the dash. "I'm really beat, man. I hope you don't mind. I need to get on home."

"Well," Bill began, the teenager again. Then his voice turned smooth. "No problem. It's only Tuesday after all."

Sam was relieved. "Yep," he nodded.

Sam got out at the corner of Seventh Avenue. The rest of the ride had been with the Will who had bantered with the cops.

"Take it easy," Bill called coolly.

Sam waved and the BMW was off like a flash.

Sam shook his head and walked toward his building. Bill was certainly full of surprises, he was thinking.

But Sam had a few himself.

Chapter Ten

Wednesday, April 12.

The morning was beautiful. So clear it seemed as if all the Jersey factories must have ceased operating. Sam's walk to work was the most enjoyable of the year.

He didn't hear from Bill all morning. Was something wrong? he wondered. But he let it pass. He didn't want to talk with Bill; he had too much to think about. And to plan.

At lunch, Sam hurried up Park Row and then, past City Hall, turned toward Chinatown and Little Italy. In a few minutes he was through the heaviest crowds, moving nonchalantly up Mulberry, where the greatest concentration of Italian restaurants was. Where Carlo's was.

Sam strolled past Carlo's once, on the opposite side of the street. He decided to walk around the block, "casing" the area as best he could. What he learned was frustrating: with all the buildings so close together, there were no obvious exits, rear or otherwise, only the front door. This was troubling.

After circling the block, Sam went into Carlo's and took a seat near the back. At 11:30, there were only a few people there. After the waiter delivered a menu, it dawned on him: this was stupid. He would be easily recognized now.

The panic lasted only a minute. Of course he would not come here again as himself. He would be in disguise. That was, after all, a great part of the excitement. He would be able to use his skills from the theater. He would create the play as necessary.

Sam stayed low-key, ordering simply, careful not to call attention to himself. And he studied the restaurant as well as he could, trying to decide where Lastretto would sit when he came in, where his men might be.

A wave of excitement rushed through him. Of course. He would come back tomorrow, Thursday. They had said Lastretto came every Thursday.

Tomorrow Sam would be here again. Only he wouldn't be Sam.

That evening, Sam began to worry because he had still not heard from Bill. He should have been more open, he guessed.

But that was probably it, he reasoned. After last night, Bill was waiting for Sam to call. He reached for the phone.

No, he told himself. No. This is right. This way you are more in control. And there was still so much planning to do. He didn't need interruptions.

With a notepad spread before him on the kitchen table, Sam began to jot down thoughts. Then he immediately scratched out everything he'd written and ripped out the page to throw away. No notes, he chided himself. Nothing written down. This will all have to be done in my head.

Sam walked to the bathroom and flushed the toilet, tearing the paper into small bits and dropping them in.

Start again, he told himself.

Disguises. An old woman. Or a young one. Sam's slender, slight build gave him a lot of flexibility. Though he could never pass for a linebacker, he could make himself into someone far more innocent looking. It was one of the things that had annoyed his wife, he guessed. His ability to get into character so easily.

And practice. He had the guns now, but he would need practice. This weekend at his uncle's upstate, of course. And that meant leaving right after work on Friday.

Tomorrow, Thursday, he would be waiting at Carlo's to get a glimpse of his victim.

CHAPTER ELEVEN

Sam was up at 4:30 setting his plans in motion. With everything in order, he walked a fast pace to work, trying to calm the excitement that threatened to overwhelm him. He would leave for lunch early, between 10:30 and 11 if he could manage it. And he was sure he could.

At 10:15, he was counting down the minutes when his phone rang, causing him to jump, so unnerved was he. Damn, he thought. He really didn't need some crap from Peter or someone.

Angrily, he snatched up the phone.

"Yeah!" he said coldly.

"Sam?" It was Bill. Damn.

"Sam, you there?"

"Uh, yeah. What's up?" He was too tense, he knew.

"Well, what're you doing?"

"Huh?" Sam was too impatient for this.

"I mean about lunch. I thought you might like to head up to Little Italy."

"Little Italy?" Sam squeaked.

There was a pause, then Bill continued, "Yes. There's a nice little place there. Carlo's."

Sam stifled his scream. What was Bill doing? How could he know? Is this the way the bold assassin handled things? Going right to the scene of the intended crime? But then, Sam was doing the same thing himself.

"Hello? Sam?"

"I'm here," Sam said a little shakily. He couldn't let anything interrupt; he had to go ahead with his plan. "Uh, look, Bill, things are a little wacko here today. I can't get away. Sorry."

"Oh," Bill responded. "Well, that's all right. We can do it some other day."

"Sure," Sam told him. "Some other day. Look, I've got to go. Talk to you later, okay?"

"Right. Later."

It was 10:30.

The wait for the No. 9 subway seemed excruciatingly long. But it was actually only about three minutes. Still Sam didn't get to his apartment until almost 10:55, and he knew he had cut the time too close.

Quickly, he changed, being careful not to rush. It would do him little good if his "character" didn't work.

The digital clock by the bed read 11:12 as Sam hurried out the door. He was definitely behind.

On the subway ride, he forced himself to calm down. Better late than to blow it. As he walked toward Carlo's, he had regained control. Sam had on his Hush Puppies with his frumpy gut disguise, padding under his loose fitting shirt and his "fat pants" from last year before he'd trimmed up. With his bushy eyebrows and sideburns and scraggly mustache, he expected to fade into the background. He took a deep breath and entered the restaurant.

Sam immediately spotted a handsome middle-aged man in

a dark suit and open shirt sitting in the back near the kitchen. He had jet-black hair with graying temples and an air of confidence. From the pictures and the description Sam had read, it had to be Lastretto.

But where were the guards?

Sam was making a quick scan of the other customers when he was interrupted by someone nearby.

"Sir?"

Sam turned toward the waiter.

"Are you meeting someone?"

Sam almost spoke before he thought, but fortunately caught himself. "No," he grunted. "Just a quiet table, please."

The waiter looked him up and down and smirked. Sam shook his head and followed the waiter to a table.

He ordered a glass of wine and took his time. It was then he realized there was a big man in a sport coat sitting near the front entrance. Anyone else who had worn a coat on this warm day had removed it and laid it across a chair, but not this man. Sam leaned back and nodded to himself.

As the waiter had already been by two more times, Sam ordered antipasto.

This time he was prepared, and pulled a paperback from his bag. He had just opened it when Sal Lastretto's meal was brought to him. Lastretto nodded at the waiter and looked over at Sam. Sam immediately returned his eyes to his book.

When he looked up again, another older man, one Sam hadn't seen before, was approaching Lastretto's table. He leaned over and the two men talked, and the standing man looked briefly in Sam's direction. Sam's heart hopped toward his throat and began to pound faster. Had they found him out?

But nothing seemed to come of it and Lastretto went ahead with his lunch. Sam continued to nibble at his antipasto, pretending to read and watching the room.

A quick movement near the door caught Sam's attention. The first man in the sport coat was on his feet as someone entered. Sam's eyes bulged. Oh, no! his brain shouted. It was Bill.

Bill, however, waited casually, his eyes gliding right past Sam's table, until the older man who had talked to Lastretto approached and led him to a table. They spoke as if they might know one another. Meanwhile, the big man near the door sat back down, but now he had both hands on the table before him.

Sam's pulse raced as he kept his eyes fixed on his book and his food. Only occasionally did he glance up to check on Lastretto and on Bill. It was far more unnerving with Bill here. Sam wanted to flee. But he kept his place, sipping his wine.

Then Lastretto was finished. The older man who had taken Bill to his table spoke with Lastretto as a waiter cleared dishes away. Sam saw Bill look slowly toward the table and ease his chair back, his right hand disappearing under his jacket.

Sam almost gasped aloud. Had Bill decided to make his move today?

Now another bulky man in a dark suit stepped from the doorway that led back to the restrooms and kitchen. It was all happening so openly and yet the other customers seemed not to notice.

As Lastretto and the bulky man passed Bill's table, Bill's hand reappeared. It held a pen and he jotted something on a matchbook cover. Lastretto and the kitchen guard met the other guard at the door and they left. Bill seemed unconcerned.

The anxiety made Sam choke on his wine, causing him to cough. For a moment, Bill looked in his direction and stared curiously, and Sam quickly buried his eyes in his book, breathing deeply. Thankfully, Bill had turned away when Sam glanced up again.

Probably no more than a minute had passed since Lastretto had left, and the episode seemed complete. Suddenly, however, Bill laid money on the table and headed for the door, leaving half-finished food and drink. Sam was caught off guard. What should he do? Follow?

Straining to see out the front window, Sam noticed a large black Mercedes pulling away from the curb. He hadn't seen it there when he came into the restaurant. Although Sam was concerned that Bill was about to spoil it all for him, Bill simply stood idly at the front counter, taking toothpicks from a dispenser. A moment later, he left without displaying any interest in Lastretto's presence.

But Sam knew it was no coincidence. He called the waiter, paid, and hurried from the restaurant in the opposite direction from Bill. He had to rush back to his apartment to change.

Sam didn't get back to the office until after 2. And by then he was quite tense, because, in addition to his lunchtime adventure, he was acutely aware that he had been gone far too long. All the way from his apartment to the office he had dreaded some confrontation with Peter, his supervisor. Now he knew he had to face it.

But there was no Peter. And no messages. By 3 o'clock he was breathing easier. As he was leaving at 4, he was relieved no one had noticed his absence.

Anne-Marie stopped him at the elevators.

"We missed you at the noon seminar, Sam."

The rug slipped from under his feet, his brain stammering for long seconds before he could get it working again.

"Oh, darn, Anne-Marie. I told you I'd be there, didn't I?"

"Yes, you did."

"I'm sorry. I had to go over and pick up these books for my mother. I can't believe I forgot." He really couldn't.

"Yeah, all right."

As the elevator doors opened, Sam tossed another "I'm sorry" and was gone. He must be more careful. But it didn't matter. None of this mattered right now.

Sam marched double-time out the front doors, his mind jumping over the events at Carlo's. The blocks clicked by almost without his realizing it. In less than a half hour, he was standing before the door to his apartment, a fog of cascading events blocking his mind.

The ringing of the phone broke his spell. Sam fumbled his key into the lock and threw the door open, rushing across the room.

"H'lo?" he sputtered.

"What's happening, Sam?"

"Bill?" Was this guy going to be on him constantly?

"You must have been in a big rush," Bill rolled on. "You almost ran over me when you zoomed out the building. I started to call after you, but, man, you were gone!"

What was Bill going on about? "What?"

"After work, Sam. I saw you heading out of the lobby."

"Oh," Sam cut in, "I remembered I had to pick up these

books for my mother."

"Your mother?"

"Yeah," Sam said. "My mother."

"Oh." Then Bill was silent. Sam regretted that he had snapped at him so quickly. He really needed time to think.

"So, what are you up to?" Bill was saying. "Hey, you sure got home quick. Where was this bookstore?"

Emotion flashed through Sam, fueled by both anger and fear. He was aggravated at Bill's questions. And apprehensive about Bill's motives. Inwardly, he took a deep breath and tried to speak calmly.

"I had called them. All I had to do was stop off and pick up the books." Then for some reason he added, "A couple of travel books."

"Yeah? Where's she going?"

"Give me a break, man," Sam half-growled at him.

Again there was a minute of silence before Bill said, "Sorry, Sam. I don't mean to be nosy."

Sam was annoyed enough that he gave no response. He was hoping to end the conversation.

"So, what are you up to this evening?" Bill asked.

"This evening?" Oh, god, thought Sam. Not tonight.

"Yeah. I know this --"

"Bill," he interrupted. "Hey, man, I'm just beat. These little errands of my mother's are a pain, and I didn't sleep much last night."

"Oh. I'm sorry, Sam. Not trying to be a nuisance."

"No, it's not you, man," Sam told him. "I mean, you've given me a lot to think about, but I'm not mad at you."

"Mad at me?"

"Yeah, I was a little curt when I answered the phone. It's all that other stuff." Then he remembered Bill's call before lunch and added, "The work stuff. And these silly things for my mother."

Neither spoke for a moment. Sam almost suggested they meet the next day for lunch. But he wanted to get away as early as possible to head upstate. And a long lunch could just make that more difficult.

"Well," said Bill quietly, "maybe we should give it a rest for a few days."

After a dead pause, Sam realized it was his turn to speak. "Yeah, Bill. I've got to do this stuff at my mother's this weekend anyway. Drop off the books, and it never ends there. Look, why don't I give you a call on Monday. Okay?"

"Sure," replied Bill, sounding unconvinced. "I need to see my mother, too. Monday's good."

Sam sighed with relief that this was not more difficult. "Okay. Talk to you Monday then."

"Yeah. Sam?"

"Yes?"

"Take it easy. Have a good weekend."

"You, too, man."

"Bye." Bill hung up.

For several minutes Sam stood staring at the phone in his hand. He hoped he hadn't screwed something up. But it sure felt like he had. Never mind, though. He had to start packing.

Sam chuckled as he dragged his suitcase out of the closet. Mothers, he smiled. They're sure handy for excuses.

CHAPTER TWELVE

The next day, Sam managed to slip away from work at 2:30. He was in by 7 in the morning and worked through lunch, hoping to get out of Manhattan before the traffic got too crazy. By 3:30 he had his car loaded and was on his way. And by 4:30, he had finally crossed the Tappan Zee Bridge and was headed upstate for real.

It was 11 by the time he got to Elmira. It was a beautiful drive, at least the daylight hours. And by dark he had left the interstate to take State Highway 17, winding through the hills, rather than stay on interstates to Binghamton. Sam could have gone straight on to the farm the other side of Elmira, but decided instead to check into a motel. He wasn't really all that interested in seeing Uncle Jack and Linda.

Carefully, he unpacked his new shotgun and rifle from the big duffel bag he'd brought to conceal them. They were lovely pieces. Sam turned the TV up high to mask any sounds and spent the next two hours loading and unloading the guns, practicing the pump action of the shotgun and aiming and pretend-firing at mock targets. It was near 2 in the morning when he regretfully put the guns away. He wanted to be fresh for tomorrow.

Sam was up and restless to go by 6. He knew Uncle Jack and Linda would be gone most of the morning on errands in town since he had indicated he wouldn't be leaving the city until Saturday morning, but it would be after 7 before they left home. This way he could avoid seeing them and go straight to the woods to test his skills.

The first time, Sam passed by their gate, checking to make sure no one was home. The truck and the car were both gone, so he turned around and headed up to the house. For several minutes he stayed in the car reorienting himself to the place after all the years since he had last been here. There was the huge barn behind the rough old house and, sure enough, the crude road past the barn that led out to the pastures and woods beyond. It was still a little muddy from the thaw, but Sam drove as far as he could before the deep ruts prevented the Camaro from proceeding farther.

He pulled to the side of the road, hauled out his duffel bag and bags from the market in town and locked the door. And chuckled at himself for such a big-city instinct that had so little meaning here. He breathed deeply and, amused and refreshed, headed off over the hill.

Sam walked for an hour. He knew Uncle Jack had more than 200 acres, with the house at the front edge, and he wanted to be as remote as possible. He zagged through woods, stepping over a lovely trickling stream, and trudged across mossy ground and over another hill. There he found his spot: a glade below, surrounded by wooded hills.

He stepped off 50 paces from the woods on the steepest hill, setting up branches and sticks at 20-, 15- and 10-pace distances from where he dropped the bag; anything farther away didn't really matter.

First he loaded the AK-47. Sam sighted in on a 3-inch

thick branch he'd set up at 20 paces. The first two shots missed, but the third one split the foot-long branch about 3 or 4 inches from the end. Not bad, he told himself. He wasn't totally out of whack. To be sure, he aimed at the shorter portion of the branch he'd just split and fired again. One shot and he struck it. The next two shots in rapid succession also hit home. Satisfaction spread in a wide smile across Sam's face. Whoever had owned this weapon before had made it a very accurate gun.

His shots at the nearer sticks hit dead on nine out of ten times. It was like electricity jolting through his veins with every shot. Finally, he loaded a new clip into the rifle and emptied the bullets as quickly as he could pull the trigger, branches and twigs hopping like popcorn.

Sam paused and listened to the contrast of the silence around him. The feelings and thoughts racing through him were impossible to explain. Except that they were good. Wondrously good.

Slowly opening the bags of groceries he'd bought in town, Sam peered at the melons and squashes. The two melons were slightly smaller than his head, the four squashes about heart-size. At distances no more than 15 feet away from his duffel, he placed the squashes on the ground, with one melon in the center. Leaving the second head-size melon on the ground off to the right a good way from the others, he returned to lug a 25-lb. bag of dog food to the spot. With a couple of branches, he braced the bag upright and, patting the top down, he set the melon on it.

The first shotgun blast not only splattered the second squash from the left, but also cut chunks from the melon a foot away. This felt good. Boom, boom, boom, he cut down the other squashes and with another quick blast, annihilated the first melon. Quickly, he reloaded before turning his attention to the last target. He wanted the gun full of shells for his "attack."

Several scenarios were discarded before Sam finally put the shotgun back in the bag. Turning his back on the melon-headed dog food bag, he partially knelt beside the duffel bag. Then with one quick motion, he grabbed the gun and swung it around. The barrel was way wide of his target.

Sam put the shotgun back in the bag and practiced his move several times with a pretend gun. When he felt he had it, he once again knelt with his back to the dog food bag. Sam quickly pulled up the shotgun, pumping a shell into the chamber as he swung around. He fired, pumped another shell, fired again and pumped a third shell.

The first shot had torn away the top right portion of the bag and destroyed half the melon. The second splattered the remainder of the melon as it flew from the bag, as well as ripping away more of the top of the bag. After the pieces had settled, he pulled the shotgun up and fired the third shot, blasting dog food nuggets all around. Then, boom-boom-boom-boom-boom!, Sam pumped off the rest of the shells as fast as he could, decimating the remainders of the bag and the ground where it had stood.

His ears were ringing and the smell of gunpowder filled his nostrils, but the feelings he had were exhilarating. The guns gave power, raw power, and he controlled it all.

In eerie silence Sam surveyed the breadth of his destruction. It was some time before the sounds of the forest resumed, but Sam hardly noticed as he was mentally mapping the interior of Carlo's Restaurant over the glade. The melon-headed bag had been Lastretto's stand-in, neutralized in seconds by quick shotgun blasts. He worried a minute about the guards. They could be anywhere. But the knowledge that his sharpshooting skill was still present filled Sam with confidence. He could do it.

Sam sat right down in the damp grass with two bath towels spread before him and lovingly cleaned his weapons. They must be in prime shape. No careless obstructions or blemishes. An hour passed before he allowed himself the luxury of drinking in the pastoral beauty of his surroundings.

The air was fresh and liquid with morning mist still evaporating from the ground as birds flitted about on their daily business. A rabbit hopped to the edge of the glade from the woods opposite Sam. He knew he could easily pull the shotgun out and destroy the creature, but he had no interest in such needless, crude pursuits. The woods belonged to the rabbit and Sam was only a visitor. He simply smiled and waved.

A little after 10, Sam shouldered his duffel bag of treasures and started back to the car. He wanted to be gone before Uncle Jack and Linda returned.

For about an hour, Sam drove along the farm roads, sticking to the paved ones. He purposefully drove through a few puddles on the road to clean mud from his tires. It all felt very intriguing, as though he were writing himself into a spy novel.

He ended on a distant hill looking down on his uncle's farm just before 1 p.m. Both vehicles were back. Sam took a deep breath and eased the Camaro down toward the driveway.

"Sam!" Uncle Jack exuded as he stomped down the steps and strode across the yard. "It's been a long time. How the hell are you?" Uncle Jack always talked like this. Another reason Sam's mother disliked him.

Linda stood on the porch, her hands folded before her, smiling broadly. She nodded approvingly as Sam and his uncle shook hands. She was so demure and kind. Sam's father had taken the family to visit them a few times when Sam was 10 to 13. Linda was quite younger than Jack and Sam had developed a teen crush on her. His heart skipped a beat just seeing her attractive face.

It was very easy to see why Uncle Jack had married this dark-skinned woman, even though it had cost him the scorn of his family.

Sam's plans to have a rather formal visit, possibly slipping away in the afternoon for more target practice, were quickly dashed. He couldn't say no to Linda. And they were just too much fun for him to consider sneaking off. They filled the afternoon and evening catching up on family news and one another's lives and laughing at Uncle Jack's outrageous stories.

It was after midnight when Sam finally got to bed, happier than he'd been in a long time.

Sunday, after a big country breakfast, they strolled around part of the property in the crisp, sunny air. Uncle Jack spoke of his connection with the land and where the country was going as Linda watched him admiringly. And Sam couldn't take his eyes off Linda. He couldn't help smiling at how different they were from his parents.

Before he knew it they were sitting down to lunch, or more like Sunday dinner at noon. By the time Sam had stuffed himself again and had dessert, it was almost midafternoon and time to start back for New York City. He had all but forgotten his original agenda. He smiled and shook hands with Uncle Jack and kissed Linda and departed, filled with regret at leaving these wonderful people.

It wasn't until he was loading his suitcase into the trunk of his car and spied the duffel that he remembered the guns. For a moment, panic welled up. But when he turned and felt Linda's warm smile, he decided it really didn't matter. He'd done what he'd come for. He'd proved he was still a sharpshooter.

Chapter Thirteen

The drive back to the city was tedious. It was always a pain on Sunday evening. It took six or seven hours to get to Elmira, then nine, maybe ten, hours to return. Sam figured himself among the thousands asking themselves the same tired question: Why do I stay in this godawful city?

He walked into his apartment a little before midnight and dropped his bags at the door. Five minutes later, the phone began ringing. Oh, no, thought Sam. My mother. She just can't leave it alone.

"Hello," he said wearily. He dreaded the sound of her voice.

"Sam, where have you --"

"Bill?"

"Yeah. I've been trying to get in touch with you."

"What's the big deal?" He barely bothered hiding his exasperation. "I told you I had to take this stuff to my mother."

"I know. But I called her."

"What!" Sam demanded. How the hell? "How did you find her number?" he almost shouted, his anger rising. It dawned on him Bill would have ample illegal resources.

"Well, it's the same last name. And you said she lived in --"

"I never said anything about where she lives!"

"You must have. And I just looked it up," Bill replied all too calmly.

Sam was beginning to panic. He knew he had never mentioned his mother's address or village to Bill. And yet, here Bill was acting like it was old information they had shared. It was bizarre.

"Sam?" Bill said to the silence in the phone. Sam stared at his harried reflection in the window across from him. Whatever was going on was not good.

He snapped out a choked response. "What?"

"You okay, man?"

Anger flashed through Sam again. "Okay? Am I okay? You spend the weekend tracking down my mother and you want to know if I'm okay?!"

"Sam," Bill said, then went silent. Sam's nostrils flared and he clenched his jaws. "My mother died Saturday morning."

Bill's statement was like a smack in the face. "What?" Sam squeaked.

"My mom died." It was such a simple sentence, delivered with no emotion or embellishment. Sam's anger had left him.

"I'm sorry, Bill." His tongue was having a rough time converting from anger to sympathy. "When? What?"

"You know. I went over to see her Friday night. She was fine. I mean, as fine as usual." Bill's words flooded from him as though they had been dammed up for days. Sam guessed they had been. "Then Saturday morning I decided to go over there again. I usually don't go on Saturday. Anyway, when I got there, it was just like usual, everyone going through their motions and all. Then I go to her room and she's not there. I just figured they'd taken her down for therapy or something, so I'd wait. Then a nurse or somebody comes up to me and asks, 'Are you a relative?' Just like that, 'Are you a relative?'

"I said, 'I'm her son. Where is she?' And she says, 'She passed away this morning.' I can't believe it. I know she was real sick, but ..."

There was a muffled sound like a sob. Sam's eyes darted around in confusion. "Bill? Are you okay?" He felt very uncomfortable with this new information, realizing he should try to help in some way.

His voice shaky, Bill said, "Yes. I'm sorry, Sam. Sorry to bother you so late and all."

"No, Bill," muttered Sam. He was still groping for words when an idea began to spread through him like a chill breeze. It was Sunday, only four days away from the hit on Lastretto and Sam still didn't have a clear plan. He just might be able to use this situation.

"Bill," he said, "why don't I come over?"

"No, Sam. It's not necessary."

"I insist. I can be there in 15 minutes. What's the address again?"

"You don't have to," Bill protested feebly.

"Bill," Sam responded quietly, "let me do this. Let me be your friend."

Bill no longer resisted. "Okay." He gave Sam the number on West 83rd.

Sam grinned in spite of himself as he hung up the phone. You're a schemer, Sam Robbins, he thought.

As he started out the door, it struck him again. How did Bill find out his mother's phone number? Who was scheming whom? Was he walking into some sort of trap?

For a moment, Sam wished very much that he had a pistol to slip into his jacket. But it was a moot point. Instead, he felt for the comfort of the Spyderco C25 Centofante knife in his right front pocket. "Gentlemen's Clipit," he scoffed at himself, and hesitated only a second before quickly turning to his closet where he pulled out a battered cardboard box. In it there was mostly junk, odd papers and old magazines and some discarded clothing. He fished around and pulled out another knife, strapped in its black leather scabbard. It was his SOG Pentagon, a short knife with a 5-inch double-edged blade, a tactical dagger. It might be just the right time for this, he decided, as he tested its weight in his hand.

Sam clipped the knife into his inside coat pocket and shoved the box back into the closet. With a little more confidence, he hurried out the door.

"Hey, Sam," said Bill as he answered Sam's knock.

Sam squeezed Bill's hand. "I'm sorry, Bill. What can I do to help?"

"You're here. That's enough." Bill did not quite smile and turned to lead Sam into the living room. "Drink?"

By Bill's unsteady walk, Sam figured he had already had several. He took whatever Bill was pouring. Scotch. Very good Scotch.

With a sigh, Bill sat on the edge of the couch. "Hell of a deal, isn't it?"

Sam nodded for Bill to go on.

"All those things. I changed my life, tried to get into a good career." Bill's eyes shot up at Sam with something akin to defensive guilt. "Not that I regret any of it. I mean, I was really going nowhere before."

To break the silence, Sam said, "But?"

"And then, she dies." This time his eyes searched Sam's pleadingly. Sam nodded again, trying to anticipate. But Bill sighed deeply and stared at the floor.

Sam walked over and laid a hand on Bill's shoulder, pausing before he spoke. "It's going to make for a tough week, isn't it? Can I do anything?"

"No. There's not really anybody. I mean, I'm all the family she's got. I'll just wrap it up tomorrow. And then ..."

Wrap it up tomorrow? wondered Sam. "And then, what?"

"Well, back to life. Taking care of business."

Sam wasn't sure, but the last statement seemed to have a chilly tone to it. Should he venture? "Maybe I could help."

Bill gave him a curious stare. "Help with what?"

But Sam held the look. "Business."

"What do you mean, Sam?" There was no appeal for sympathy in the way Bill said it.

Sam removed his hand from Bill's shoulder before he started shaking. As calmly as he could, he turned his back and walked over to the bottle to refill his glass. "Whatever it is you do on the side," he said calmly, fixing steely eyes on Bill.

Cocking his head boyishly, Bill replied, "Well, thanks, Sam, but there's not really anything."

Sam's nerve was sliding quickly away, so he returned with, "Maybe something with your mother. I could help."

"I'll take care of it tomorrow," Bill said in a cool, business voice. "Just a phone call. Cremation. It's done in a day."

Sam's mouth hung open as he stared. He had definitely let his grip slip. He had to do something to ease Bill's suspicions. Sheepishly, he lowered his eyelids.

"I'm really sorry, Bill."

By the look in Bill's eyes, he knew it had worked. "Thanks for coming over, Sam," Bill managed. "I didn't mean to get so tense a couple of minutes ago. I just --"

"Forget it, man," Sam told him. "It's not a good time to be hassling someone."

"No, you weren't --"

"No. I wasn't. But I guess it sounded a little like it. I just wanted to help."

They stared at one another. Sam's heart thumped loudly. He had no idea what Bill could be thinking. He only hoped his nervousness didn't show.

Bill finally broke the silence. "You look a little tense."

Sam flinched, but he hoped Bill couldn't tell. "These silences always make me nervous." Say as little as possible, he commanded himself. Until you're back in control.

"Yeah," said Bill. He turned his gaze to his near-empty glass and downed the remaining Scotch. Extending his glass, he said, "Fix me another?"

"Sure." When Sam reached to take the glass, Bill's fingers locked around his, causing Sam a second of panic. Quickly, though, he responded with a warm smile, pulling the glass free. As he filled it, he said, "I'm sorry I wasn't there. When you called this weekend." He turned his best hurt look to Bill and handed him the drink.

"No, it's all right," Bill said quietly. "And don't worry. I didn't say anything to get your mom excited. Just said I was an old school chum."

Sam smiled. "Even that will probably get her excited."

With a chuckle, Bill turned a serious face to Sam. "What's it take to get you excited?"

Sam had to scramble for an answer. With studied coyness, he said, "I think you might have some idea. Mystery. Adventure."

"Those are forms of excitement."

"The things associated with them. I'm just a red-blooded male."

"Meaning, a hot-blooded female?"

Sam answered with a wry half-smile. "Meaning man things. Hunts. Weapons. Action. Chasing and racing."

"You seemed a little scared by the racing the other night."

Carefully calculating the level of flirtation, Sam said, "Not so much the racing as where the heck we were going."

"The mystery," Bill grinned.

"Maybe you were a little scary."

"Maybe I am."

Sam had an almost uncontrollable urge to tell Bill all about his weekend upstate, but he caught himself. This was not the time. Bill had in no way revealed himself, his other life. Not since the night he had gotten so drunk.

Sam looked down at his watch and said, "I've got to go."

"You could stay here."

Bill was still several steps ahead of him, keeping Sam rattled. This could be his chance, but Sam wasn't sure he could handle it. Finally, he pulled his gaze away from his watch to Bill's eyes. "Okay."

As Bill smiled and rose to walk toward him, Sam's heart began to pound so hard he thought surely Bill could hear. And maybe he could, for he reached straight to the left side of Sam's chest.

"Why don't you take your coat off and relax," said Bill, touching Sam's lapel.

In his moment of panic, Sam searched wildly for some image to help him. And found it. He remembered his wife approaching him in the same manner when she wanted something from him -- he must help her get the female lead in the play he was in, he should work overtime so she could buy new clothes. Always when she wanted something. Quickly, his blood began to chill. He grasped Bill's hand with his own left hand and lowered it, all the while locking onto Bill's eyes.

"Pour me another Scotch?" he purred, placing his glass in Bill's hand.

"Of course," Bill nodded confidently.

Sam realized as Bill turned away that with just a little more pressure on his coat, Bill would have felt the handle of the knife in Sam's inside pocket. Sam couldn't help smiling.

He crossed to the other end of the room and peered out the curtains as ice clinked into their glasses. More Scotch? He was already dizzy. But only partly from the alcohol, he admitted.

Bill was way ahead of him on the drinks, but he also seemed to have a way of handling it very well. Far better than Sam. So this gave Sam no advantage. At least not yet.

"Show me your place," he said with his back still to Bill. "This is the only room I've been in."

As Sam turned toward him, Bill raised both eyebrows and, with a faint grin, said, "Follow me."

Bill showed him first to the bedroom, decorated in dark colors with black bedspread and curtains and dark blue walls, but lots of lights. The low-standing black lacquered oriental dresser held a huge mirror, probably 4 feet square. Mirrors also covered the floor-to-ceiling doors of the closet on the adjacent wall. There was a door opposite the closet, but Bill ignored it.

Next was the bathroom, with large mirrors, bright lights and, again, black curtains on the shower and black rugs covering the carpet.

The last room Sam took to be an office. Two black wooden chests with large drawers, looking something like filing cabinets, were on the far wall between two doors. Closets, Sam guessed, but again, Bill didn't open them. On another wall was a small, dark brown couch, oddly out of place with the room and its colors.

"Very nice," said Sam as they stepped back to the hallway.

"I'm not finished yet," Bill told him. He opened a door so well blended into the wall Sam had missed it. "Come on," Bill said as he started up a flight of stairs.

"This is my playroom," he announced with a sweep of his hand.

Sam's mouth dropped open with both amazement and amusement. The entire second floor was one large room. The ceiling was perhaps 20 or 25 feet high. A basketball goal was mounted on the back wall; weights and exercise equipment were arranged in order along another wall. The floor was all hardwood, with rugs and padded mats here and there. And on the wall to his left hung a shiny dark-green mountain bike, some archery equipment and a very long canoe.

"How do you get the canoe down those stairs?" Sam frowned.

With a chuckle, Bill said, "I don't. I take it down the back way." He walked to the right from the entrance and opened double doors revealing a wide stairway. "To the garage," he said to Sam's unasked question.

All Sam could think was, This place must cost a lot of

bucks. Sam's whole apartment could fit in one end of Bill's gymnasium.

So dazzled was he, Sam almost didn't hear Bill asking, "Shoot a few baskets?"

"Huh," Sam muttered, turning slowly.

Bill dribbled the basketball a couple of times and suddenly fired it straight at him. Sam barely recovered in time to catch it. "Right. Okay." He shot from where he stood, 15 feet from the goal, and the ball bounced off the rim.

"Not bad," said Bill smugly. "Good distance, but no score."

Raising his left eyebrow to the challenge, Sam took off his coat and dropped it on the floor with a thunk.

"Too much crap in my wallet," he quickly said.

"Sounded like a lead pipe."

Ignoring the implication, Sam ran to cover Bill. "Cheap, fat wallet. Make your shot."

Bill stared at him for just an instant, then spun quickly to his left, drawing Sam out, and broke toward the basket. He was up and had the ball through the hoop in a flash.

"Yeah!" he smirked.

"Well, it's your gym."

"And my ball. Come on, kiddo, let's play."

Deliberately picking up the basketball in slow motion, Sam swooped in and shot, the ball just touching the rim as it whisked through.

"I'm not sure that was fair," said Bill, walking forward for the rebound.

"What's fair?" Sam replied and rushed to guard Bill's next move.

"No turnabout's fair play?"

"Nope," grinned Sam. This time he blocked Bill's shot and they both laughed.

Back and forth they went for several minutes, neither of them managing to score another basket. Sam was breathing hard, but he was keeping pace.

"Hey," Bill panted, "you're in pretty good shape."

"For an office rat?" Sam said, slapping the ball away from Bill's hands. "Why wouldn't I be in as good shape as you?"

"Well, I work out here." Sam blocked his shot again.

"I run almost every day," Sam told him, "and I run the --" He almost said "stairs" but caught himself. He faked a gasp for air to continue with, "I run the distance from work on some days, too."

"That would explain it. That doesn't explain your shooting, though."

"What shooting? I haven't made a basket in 10 tries."

"Well, neither have I. And it's my game, remember?"

"Your gym," Sam corrected.

"Yeah, right." Bill used the moment to fake a move to the right and then shoot left to the basket. The ball swished through.

"Perfect shot," Sam congratulated. He braced his hands on his knees to catch his breath and looked at his watch: 2:30.

"Hey," he said, stretching, "I'm going to have to go."

"I thought you were going to stay here," said Bill, making it sound like a question. There was obvious disappointment in his voice.

"Well, yeah, but here I am playing basketball. I've got to get to work early tomorrow. Today."

"You could just consider this your morning run."

"What makes you think I'm alive enough to run in the mornings?" Sam kidded. "But really," he said, looking deep into Bill's eyes, "thanks a lot, but I need to get on home."

Bill was silent. Then he rolled the ball to the corner and said, "Okay, man." He waited, as if allowing the ball to settle, before turning to Sam. "Thanks for coming. It was real good of you."

Sam nodded and started for the stairs.

At the front door, Bill offered to call a cab, but Sam declined. "I'll just take the subway. It's a nice night."

"I'll walk with you," Bill said. Sam didn't resist.

As they turned the corner and walked silently down Central Park West, Sam could sense Bill's awkwardness. Bill was like a kid wondering if he should hold the girl's hand or not. He was about to break the quiet when someone angling across the street from the park hailed them.

"Hey."

Sam ignored him and so did Bill.

"Hey, man, I'm talking to you," the man challenged.

"What?" said Sam with surprise.

But Bill didn't seem at all put off. "Surely you don't mean us, do you?"

"Yeah, mother," the guy barked, his hand shooting out deliberately, something in his hand reflecting the streetlights.

It was all so fast, Sam hardly knew what was happening. Bill quickly reached past Sam, grabbing the man's arm. Then, pushing Sam aside with his left shoulder, he spun toward the man and somehow pulled him to the right, away from Sam. Sam heard a deep grunt from the man as Bill's right knee hit something solid very hard. In an instant, the man and his knife were sprawled across the sidewalk, just after Bill had managed to kick him once in the face on the way down.

"What the hell?!" Sam finally found his voice.

"Idiot," Bill said, staring down at the still form. He'd hardly raised his voice. "Come on," he continued, taking Sam's arm. "Let's get out of here."

They'd gone another block or so, with Sam looking back twice to be sure what had happened, before he could speak again. They had almost reached the subway station.

"Man, how the heck did you do that? Did you know this guy? I could hardly tell what was happening, even with plenty of light back there," Sam blurted out all at once.

Bill stood with a bemused look. "I just kicked his ass. That's all."

"Kicked more than his ass," Sam replied, still in awe.

Bill shrugged. "Just a few moves I learned."

"In your other line of work?" Sam retorted. He immediately wondered if he shouldn't have said it.

Bill seemed surprised at the comment, but then he smiled. "I guess you could say that."

They were both silent. Bill's smile faded and the awkwardness seemed upon them again. Clearing his throat, Sam said, "Thanks."

"No problem," said Bill, staring first at the ground and then raising his eyes to Sam. "I --"

"Bill --"

"What?"

"Thanks," Sam said, extending his hand. Bill gripped it, their handshake lasting a very long moment.

"Good night," Sam told him. "See you later?" He turned to

start down the steps to the subway.

"Come on, man," said Bill. "Let's get you a cab."

Sam laughed. "No argument."

Moments later Sam was on his way as Bill stood and watched him disappear.

CHAPTER FOURTEEN

Five o'clock Monday morning.

Sam lay in his bed drifting in and out of sleep, hearing distant voices broken by brief strains of music.

"Traffic and weather together on the eights on News Radio 88. Midtown tunnel --"

Sam's eyes snapped open to stare at the clock. He started to sit up but dropped his head back on the pillow.

"Ohhh." Three hours sleep? Or was it two and a half? "Forget the run," muttered Sam as his left hand went down to pull up the covers. He could sleep until 8.

"Ugh. Get up," he sighed. The Scotch dragged at his gut as he climbed into the shower. Sam had just soaped his face when the water went icy cold.

"Yo!" he gasped. Then he growled, "Damn him." The so-called new boiler he was paying a $20 surcharge for each month continued to plague the tenants. With all its "new electronic controls," if Raul was not there at 4:30 every morning to turn the crank, they had no hot water. And this morning, Raul was dependable as ever.

"Braagh," Sam bellowed as he hurriedly soaped and rinsed. He was definitely awake now.

Just as well. He needed his morning run. A lot of thinking and planning before Thursday.

At least the hot water was finally on by the time he got back and Sam showered quickly, fearing it might disappear again.

The morning muddled by at work, Sam constantly gazing through the windows at the gray day settling in. He skipped his walk on the stairs and by lunchtime, he regretted it, for the gray sky had turned to rain. The long walk along the river Sam had anticipated would have to wait. By afternoon the rain was really coming down, so Sam was relegated to taking the subway, crowded more than usual and smelling of wet clothing and hair.

When he got home, he was soaked from the three-block walk from the station and decided to chance the shower again. He was blessed with hot water, which improved his mood, but he was still gripped by a great restlessness. Munching on an apple and a carrot, he paced the apartment, trying to focus on Thursday. He stopped before the short stack of videotapes next to his VCR.

He grappled with indecision, then grabbed a tape.

"One more time," he said out loud.

Impatiently, Sam fast-forwarded past the title and the beginning and stopped just after Jamie Lee Curtis shot the bad guy and the large pistol lay on the floor of the deli, the soon-to-be killer staring down at it. It was a question Sam himself was facing. But when the man grabbed it, Sam smiled. He knew he could do this.

The movie continued, but Sam was no longer paying attention. Instead he was going over his makeup and clothing disguise for Thursday and rehearsing the route to Carlo's. Absentmindedly, he turned the sound off and began to pace, staring out the window at what sky he could see. He could not pull himself from his reverie. Until the videotape came to an end and the VCR automatically ejected it with a whirring click. Sam turned to look at it, captivated. Then he pushed the tape back in and hit "rewind." On the silent TV people were spinning a great roulette wheel for prizes amid much waving of hands and foolish looks.

As if on cue from the spinning wheel, Sam's mind clicked into place. He walked to the bedroom closet and pulled out the duffel bag with the shotgun and AK-47 in it. He laid them out on the floor to admire, gently passing his hands along the dull, cold barrels and stocks. With a feeling of resolve, he picked up the shotgun and threw himself into cleaning it.

After the shotgun, he cleaned the AK-47. Then he took stock of his ammunition. Satisfied, he put it all back in the bag.

For good measure, he pulled out the boxes with his makeup and costume clothing, and once more reviewed the route to Carlo's and the timing involved. He would make a dry run, a dress rehearsal, tomorrow.

The phone was ringing.

Sam looked at his bedside clock: 10:05. It wouldn't be his mother. He started toward the phone. Six rings, eight, as he stood there.

"H'lo!" he spat.

Silence, then a click. Annoyed, Sam hung up.

Just as he was about to turn off the TV, the ringing started again.

Three rings and Sam grabbed the phone. "What?" he almost growled.

"Sam?"

Sam grimaced. It was Bill.

"Hey, what's up?" Sam muttered hollowly.

A pause and Bill said, "You okay?"

"Yeah. Why wouldn't I be?"

"Did I catch you at a bad time?"

Patience, Sam told himself. He's your friend. And you still need him.

Cars zoomed down the streets of some nondescript city on TV, a chase scene. "I'm just tired. I was zoned out in front of the TV." For effect, he added, "What time is it?"

"About a quarter after 10. I called once and didn't get an answer. Guess I woke you up then, since you answered when I called right back." Bill seemed pleased with himself. Which irritated Sam.

"Yeah, I guess so," he said.

"Sorry," was Bill's reply. Then he was quiet.

Sam struggled for the sense of this conversation, tempted to just hang up. "What's up?" he repeated.

"Oh, just winding down after the day. I got the things done."

What is he going on about, Sam wondered. And suddenly it hit him. Bill's mother. The cremation arrangements. He felt like an ass.

"Hey, that's good," he said.

"Yeah. Good to have it taken care of," Bill replied.

Sam pondered another late night visit with Bill. He just wasn't up to it and fumbled for some way to explain. "Well --"

"Sorry to wake you, Sam," Bill interrupted. "I just wanted to say good night. And, thanks. Thanks a lot for being here, Sam."

"Yeah, sure."

"I really mean it. Now get some sleep, man."

"Yeah. You, too."

"Good night." The phone clicked.

For a moment Sam stood holding the phone in his hand. Then hung it up. Okay, he thought. Good. I do need to get some sleep.

He put the guns away in the back of the closet and boxed up his costuming. Only a few hours away, he told himself. A new world.

He crawled into bed and fell quickly to sleep.

CHAPTER FIFTEEN

He was awake at 4:33. Before the radio came on.

Gone was the numb shakiness he had experienced yesterday after the Sunday night Scotch. But there was no denying the jittery feeling in his stomach. It was the same as he felt every time before he went out onstage. And this was his biggest role yet.

Again he thought of taking the day off. But, no. It wouldn't work. It had to be like any other day. Maybe Thursday; he hadn't decided yet.

A good run didn't quell his excitement much, but he did feel more focused. He prayed for a smooth morning. But, if anything had to go wrong, make it today or tomorrow. Please. Not Thursday.

The mundane office work and idle chatter was easier than he expected. Then there it was, 10:45. He was still free. He wouldn't wait any later for something to come up. Sam slipped out unnoticed.

11 o'clock and he was home.

Sam hurried through applying his makeup and getting his costume together. Today, he would be the old lady. Same as on Thursday. This was, after all, the dress rehearsal for the real show.

No need to haul along the guns today, but he did load a

few boxes on his little-old-lady's grocery cart. Fortunately, he was able to slip out of his building without so much as being noticed.

At Seventh Avenue, he grabbed a taxi to Little Italy. Time was too close to walk, but he got out at Grand Avenue and Centre Street. From there it was an easy couple of blocks to Mulberry and down to Carlo's.

It was almost 11:40 when he arrived. The place was pretty quiet. No guards, and no Lastretto, of course. Sam as the little gray-haired lady pulled the cart of packages over to a table and sat down, not waiting for a waiter.

One arrived soon enough, though, and slapped a glass of water on the table. Sam stopped him short.

"You mind wiping this table, young man?"

"Excuse me?" the waiter said.

"Wipe the table. It's got dust on it."

The waiter rolled his eyes. "Sure," he muttered and sauntered over to the bar. In a moment he was back with a damp rag and a surly expression and made a few quick whisks over the table.

"Okay?"

Sam smiled, enjoying his role. "Thank you. Now would you mind drying it?" he said as the waiter started to turn away.

The man stopped, frowned and used his white apron to dry the tabletop. "There. Satisfied?"

"I will be if you'll bring me a menu."

With a flourish, the waiter laid a menu before the aggravating woman and walked away, shaking his head.

Sam studied the menu, refusing to look up when someone, the waiter he supposed, came to stand by the table. Then a chair pulled out and the man sat down. It was not the waiter.

Sam looked up quickly, genuinely surprised.

"Good day, madame. My boy seems to think you're giving him trouble."

Sam caught himself from bursting out angrily in his normal voice and the little old lady demanded, "What!"

"Hahaha," the elderly man laughed in a melodious tenor. Then lowering his voice, he said, "He's a young punk. What can I say?"

"How about saying to him to get over here and take my order?"

"Haha," the melody rolled again. "Never mind about him. I'll take your order. I'm happy to be of service to a lovely lady like you."

"I beg your pardon," the old lady snapped.

"How can I serve you," the man smiled mischievously.

With cold eyes, the old lady said, "You can bring me some soup."

"Certainly, madame," he said rising. "Our best minestrone."

In a few minutes he was back with a large steaming bowl of soup, set it before the lady and remained, smiling down.

Sam looked up, as he'd seen his mother do on so many occasions, and said, "That will be all."

The man turned and ambled away.

But he returned shortly with a carafe of red wine. He poured a glass and set it before the lady and then poured a second glass.

"I didn't order that."

"Courtesy of the management."

"But --"

"To make up for the rude young waiter."

"And the second glass?" she asked carefully.

"Just a glass for your admiring servant."

"And who would that be?"

"Why, me, of course."

"Of course," she snapped. "Take it away."

"But, madame," he said, seating himself with a wide smile and reaching over to lay a well-manicured hand on her sleeve, "we can get to be fine friends."

"You will leave this instant or I will call the manager," said the lady sternly.

"I am the manager."

"Then I will speak to the owner."

"Allow me to introduce myself. Carlo Vitole at your service," he said, reaching a second time for her hand.

"I don't have to stand for this. I'm sure you won't be so smug if I tell --"

"Tell whom?" he grinned.

"Salvatore Lastretto," the lady blurted out.

Immediately, the man's smile, and most of his color, faded. "L-Lastretto?"

"Yes. Sal Lastretto."

"But, surely, madame," he stammered, "this is all in good friendship. Mr. Lastretto comes here often. A very good customer."

"And a friend of mine."

"Yes. Yes, I see." He had become all business.

Resisting the urge to smile, Sam continued, "Now leave my table."

"Uh, certainly, madame. No offense, I assure you," he said, quickly rising.

"And ..." Sam could not resist.

"Yes?"

"Leave the wine."

"Surely. It's on the house."

"Why thank you, young man," she smiled.

Carlo turned and disappeared into the kitchen.

Slowly, Sam supped the soup, marveling at Carlo's quick change. He almost chuckled to himself until he glanced at his watch: 12:35. He needed to go.

"Excuse me," said the prim lady Carlo had admired. "I need the check please."

The waiter standing by the bar nodded and went into the kitchen. In a moment, Carlo reappeared.

"Please. There is no check. You are our guest."

"I'll be in no one's debt," said the woman. She fished in her coat pocket and brought out a $5 bill, laying it on the table. "This should do. I didn't order the wine, after all."

"No, madame. I assure you --"

"Thank you," she said brusquely as she rose. Taking her cart, she marched out the front door.

Sam could barely contain himself for the next block. Finally, when he turned the corner, he let out a chuckle. Then a most unladylike loud hahaha. The play had gone well. And Carlo's reaction to "Sal Lastretto" had been priceless. He took a cab back to near his apartment, rushed up and made a quick change and hurried down to the subway. He was at his desk before 1:45.

The rest of the afternoon he spent trying to calm down. But it was nearly impossible to ease the excitement he was feeling. By 3, though, he was caught up in a couple of work problems, trouble with some office space in one of the buildings. It took some wrangling to get things settled and when he finally pushed away from his computer, it was 5:30.

Sam smiled to himself. How time flies when you're having fun.

Chapter Sixteen

Sam felt as if he flew home, his mind was racing so. Inside he was pacing around the apartment congratulating himself and planning ahead to Thursday. Several times his eyes passed over the videotapes, but he told himself: I don't need that now.

Perhaps he shouldn't have come so close to Carlo. But he hadn't really had any choice, had he? He would be recognized for sure now if he wore the same costume. But why not? Yes, Carlo had bought it. And maybe that would be even better.

Sam was so antsy he couldn't stay cooped up in the apartment. With only a moment's consideration, he rushed out. He would get something to eat and he would walk.

The weather was beautiful. One of those fine April evenings that remind more of the warmth of May. The streets were full of life and spring was definitely in the air. Sam felt such elation that he could hardly stop in one place long enough to eat. He bought two hotdogs from a street vendor and headed for Washington Square, where he strolled and watched people as he ate.

Dark seemed to draw out even more people. Sam was charged. It was good to be in New York on this spring evening.

It was after 10 when he returned to his apartment, his legs a bit worn from all the walking. He must have gone a dozen miles so far. He grabbed a large glass of water and dropped into the living room chair with a great breath of relief. Sure, Thursday was going to be different. Thursday was the real thing. But Sam felt real good about it.

After he finished the water, Sam relaxed. He closed his eyes. Inhaling deeply, he exhaled slowly. And began to drift. In a few minutes, he saw himself running. He was carrying the shotgun, bent low and crossing arid hills. There was no one chasing him; it was more like he was stalking.

When Sam opened his eyes, it seemed very still and quiet. Distant sounds of traffic drifted up to him, but they were muted. Slowly, his mind focused, then his eyes. Sam looked at his watch: 1:30.

With some effort he rose on his sore feet and stumbled to the bedroom. He had stripped off his clothes and climbed into bed before he remembered: What had happened to Bill? He hadn't even called. Or had he? Sam had been gone all evening.

No matter, he told himself. Tired. Tomorrow.

When his eyelids fluttered, Sam sensed something different. He raised his head from the pillow and forced his eyes open to the bright light. Was that what was different?

Slowly, his gaze turned toward the clock: 7:47.

"Damn!" he swore. He had forgotten to set the alarm. He was usually at work by 7:30. And here it was the day that --

No. No, it was only Wednesday, not Thursday yet. At least there was that relief.

Sam threw back the covers and headed for the shower. Thankfully, the water was hot. There was that advantage to getting up late.

And it wasn't so bad. He was at work by 8:45, earlier than a lot of people in his office.

Concentrating on work was near impossible, though. So much to think about. And just one more day until his grand performance. A lot of people were going to be very surprised. He hoped he wasn't one of them.

Now how was he going to deal with Bill and actually take over the assignment?

By lunchtime, he thought he had it figured out. Sam picked up the phone and called Bill.

"H'lo."

"Bill?"

A pause and Bill said, "Is that you, Sam?"

"Yeah. How you been? Sorry I flaked out Monday night."

"Naw, that's all right. You needed your beauty rest."

"Well, I'm sure I could use a lot more of that. Not near as beautiful as I should be."

No response from Bill, so Sam said, "Quite the opposite last night. I was so restless I went out walking and didn't get back till late."

"Ah," said Bill.

"You all right, man?"

"Yeah. Look, I got a lot of work --"

"Did you try to call last night?"

"I ... No problem, man."

Sam couldn't help but grin at this guy behaving like a snubbed sweetheart. But he needed to think of something quick.

"Hey, I can see you're busy," said Sam. "Can we get together after work? For dinner or something?"

Again a pause. Sam worried what was going through Bill's mind. Maybe he was already getting himself mentally prepared for tomorrow's hit. Maybe --

"Sure, okay. See you after work then."

"What time you working to?"

"Uh, 5. No, 4:30."

"Good," Sam replied. "See you in the lobby. At 4:30."

"Right. Bye." And he hung up.

Sam wasn't sure what to make of it. Bill had seemed so friendly earlier in the week. Now it was like trying to get the guy to meet with his insurance agent. He would have to be very careful about putting his plan into action.

At a quarter to 5, Sam stood in the lobby, but still no Bill. He paced across the length of the lobby again; maybe Bill was taking an elevator on the other end (even though Sam could easily see him if he did).

Elevators opened and people poured out. It was almost 5 now. Why was he so nervous? Better get a grip if everything was going to work.

At 5:04, there was Bill, slowly ambling off an elevator on the opposite end, where Sam had started out waiting. Anxiously, he hurried to meet Bill.

Bill was looking drawn, tired. "Sorry," he said. "I got tied up on this damn project."

"You said 4:30."

"I know. I'm really sorry." And he truly seemed so.

Sam decided he might use this to his advantage. "Come on," he said.

Dinner was quiet. Bill seemed preoccupied. As if I'm not,

Sam thought. Still, Sam had determined his plan.

"So, Bill, you okay?"

"What?" Bill looked up. "Oh, sure."

Sam took a silent deep breath and reached over and touched Bill's hand. "What's the problem, man? Did I do something wrong?"

Though Bill didn't move his hand, Sam felt Bill's muscles tighten ever so slightly. And Bill's slowness in answering made it apparent he was nervous or uncomfortable. But about what, Sam was not sure.

"Sam, look, I," Bill began. He slipped his hand from under Sam's and gripped the edge of the table. "I've behaved foolishly. I've been a jerk."

Sam looked at him, not believing this. Not now, he wanted to shout. It's been going so well. Instead, he said, "What do you mean?"

"Oh, having you come over and crowding you. I've been --"

"Bill, this is nuts," Sam said.

"But you, I mean --"

"Bill," Sam said, lowering his voice, "we've had a good time together, haven't we? I mean, except for the zooming through unsavory parts of Brooklyn and scaring the hell out of me." He grinned as confidently as he could.

Bill's weak smile was not much encouragement, but Sam hurried on. "I admit I was a little unsure in the beginning. I'm not exactly good with making friends." He dropped his eyes coyly.

"But we had a good time. And I thought," Sam trailed off, giving Bill his best hurt expression.

Bill only looked at him, his eyebrows drawing together in a

pained frown. He opened his mouth and his lips searched for a moment before he spoke. "Yes, we did have a good time. I was just afraid maybe I was misreading things."

Sam watched him carefully. The time was right. Quietly, he said, "Why don't we leave here and go up to your place. Where we can relax and have a drink and just talk. Without all this." He nodded his head toward the people at other tables.

Bill sat back as if to assess the request and then replied just as quietly, "Okay."

The evening was so beautiful that Sam yearned to walk, but he didn't want to lose the moment. Right away he hailed a cab.

The ride was in near silence except for the jarring Middle-Eastern music from the driver's radio. Sam was pondering his moves and Bill seemed unsure. Sam had the driver stop on Broadway at 80th and paid him before Bill could react.

"Let's walk a little," he said after they were out of the cab. Sam's planning was making him cautious about where he was seen.

It was just a 10-minute walk to Bill's place, but their silent stroll took 15 minutes. Sam's heart pounded as he considered whether he was making the right move. And he hoped he was prepared for the evening. He thought he was.

Once inside, he waited while Bill poured drinks, his reliable Scotch.

"Thanks," he told Bill and tipped his glass. "To a pleasant evening."

Bill seemed more at ease now, as Sam had expected. Bill smiled comfortably, nodded to the toast and took a long drink. Sam was pleased with himself so far.

"Look, it's been a stressful week," said Sam. "Especially for you. With your mother's passing and all. And then these past few days, maybe we ran up the hill a little fast. But it has been okay, hasn't it? I mean for the most part?"

Bill nodded and said, "Yes. You're right. They were some days of extremes. And I thought maybe after Monday night and the guy in the street, you were a little freaked or something."

Frowning at him, Sam said, "What? No way. I was impressed. Big-time movie badass," he grinned.

"Well, it's not quite --"

"Aw, you're too modest," Sam told him as he studied Bill. "Let me fix you another drink," he said, rising. "And maybe you can tune in some music."

He took Bill's glass and turned away, feeling barely able to hide how scared he was.

With his back to Bill, he looked around to make sure Bill was occupied, flipping through CDs. He took a bottle from his pocket, poured a little Scotch in Bill's glass and then shook in some of the white powder from the bottle. More Scotch and a little more powder.

Sam's pulse was racing. He didn't see a spoon, so he stirred the drink with his finger. It began to foam slightly and Bill startled him with "You like the old Eagles? I've got several. I could show you."

"No," said Sam, a little too quickly. He gritted his teeth and clenched his eyes a fraction of a second and let out a breath, forcing himself to turn slowly. "I like them all," he said calmly. "How about the one with 'Desperado' on it?"

Bill nodded and returned to the CDs. He hadn't appeared to notice Sam's moment of panic.

The Scotch had stopped fizzing and Sam smelled it. Seemed

fine. He tasted a drop from his finger. Okay.

The music started as Sam handed Bill the drink. Bill had programmed the stereo to play "Desperado" first. How appropriate, Sam grinned. He picked up his own drink and held it up in salute. "Down the hatch," he said.

Bill nodded and slugged the Scotch down. It couldn't have gone better.

Sam watched him, sipping on his own drink. Though Bill was frowning down into his glass, it appeared to be because the drink was almost empty. But Sam didn't want any suspicions now.

"Maybe we can just relax again," he said. "Like we were a few days ago. The tension of the last couple of days is history, okay?"

Shaking the loose ice in his glass, Bill returned Sam's gaze. "All right."

With a relieved smile, Sam rose. "Fine," he said. "Get you another one?"

"Thanks."

As Sam took the glass, Bill held the grip a moment. "You're a real pal, Sam. I appreciate it."

"No problem. Scotch, is it?" he kidded.

"Uh, yeah," Bill feigned. "That sounds fine. I'll just take a quick rest stop, all right?"

"See you," Sam said.

As he started to pour more Scotch, Sam thought, What the heck? Bill's out of the room a couple of minutes, so I might as well add a little more. He wasn't sure of the effects, but why not? Leaning back and taking a quick glance down the hall, Sam pulled out the little bottle and shook more white powder into the glass. More than he'd intended, but he quickly put the lid on, dropped the bottle in his pocket and swirled the drink.

For a moment he thought he'd go around to the sink and dump it down the drain as it fizzed away. But Bill wasn't back and the fizzing was stopping. He dipped his finger in and tasted. Was that a little bit of bitterness?

"Might as well top yours off, too," Bill said, coming up the hallway.

Sam jumped, surprised. "Uh, yeah. Why not. Here you go," he said, picking up his own glass. "I guess I'll make that little stop, too."

"Just on the right there," Bill told him.

Sam walked down the hall, taking his drink with him.

When he came back, Bill had loosened his shirt and was sprawled on the floor in front of the sofa. His head was tilted back and he stared at the ceiling holding his near-empty glass before him. His head wobbled toward Sam and he said, "Hey."

The quantity of Scotch alone should have done this, thought Sam, so he could only wonder about the effect of his additive. Still, he took Bill's glass and went to pour him another.

He realized then that Bill must have already had another while Sam was in the bathroom, for the bottle was almost empty. Draining the last of the Scotch, Sam said, "You got more?"

"Sure," said Bill. "Ish in the boddle ... uh, the ... cabinet. Other side ... door."

Walking around the counter to the kitchen, Sam looked up, then down. "Cabinet above or below?" he asked.

"Iss ... b'low," Bill replied with some effort.

Sam tried a couple of doors and found the stash, a whole

row of fresh bottles. As he pulled one out and broke it open, he frowned over at Bill whose head was bobbing down to his chest. Sam worried that he had overdone it, used too much of the powder. Still, Sam was surprised that Bill was able to function with the liquor he put away.

Though it seemed pointless, he poured the drink. He walked over and set it on the coffee table and stood staring down at Bill. Was the guy gone? Did it act this fast?

"Bill?"

No response.

"Hey, Bill," he said as he gently shook the other man's head.

Bill's chin dropped to his chest. "Mmmm."

Sam sat on the sofa, his hands on his knees, unsure -- now that the time was here -- what to do. His heart began to beat faster as he felt himself entering into a world he'd fantasized about. This is it, the real deal, he told himself. It's not a movie this time. Biting his lip, he looked again at Bill. He swallowed and tried again.

"Bill. Hello?"

Bill didn't stir.

"Come on, man. Let's get you to bed." Sam started to pull Bill up but Bill had gone limp and simply rolled over to the floor. With concern, Sam reached over and lifted Bill's wrist to take his pulse.

Relieved, he sat back on the sofa again. Bill obviously was thoroughly passed out. But now what? Did he drag him to the bedroom?

Sam stood up. Perhaps it didn't matter right now. Bill obviously wasn't going anywhere. Nor was he in any condition to hinder Sam.

To reassure himself, Sam knelt and patted Bill's cheeks lightly in an effort to rouse him. Bill moaned slightly. Okay, thought Sam. From his pocket he pulled a pair of surgical gloves and slipped them on. Then he switched off the stereo and headed down the hall to the bedroom.

He turned and looked one more time at Bill and flipped on the light.

Sam pulled open drawers in the chest. Each contained neatly folded clothes and carefully arranged personal items. Nothing to help. Sam turned to the near closet and found nothing there but clothes and shoes. The second closet was deeper and contained bed linens, blankets, towels. All ordinary household goods. He even looked under the bed.

Flipping off the light, Sam checked to see that Bill had not moved and headed for the second room, the office.

First he went through the desk. Papers, office supplies, some current bills. Sam pulled the American Express bill from its envelope and scanned it: $3,758. Clothes, restaurants -- the guy knew how to live. He folded it away and put it back in the desk.

Next, the file cabinet. Paid bills, tax records, paycheck stubs. Sam pulled out the most recent stubs. Tax, insurance deductions; net pay: $2,633.17. That was less than Sam made.

The other drawers contained travel materials, vacation information. And a few catalogs of military surplus items.

Sam stood in the middle of the room thinking. The closet was the last place to look. He first went up the hall to see Bill still passed out where he had been, then returned and opened the closet door.

It was a big, walk-in closet. There was luggage and a few

briefcases. Sam tried a couple of them and they were locked, but seemed empty.

At one end of the closet was a large, shallow chest of drawers that stood about 4 feet high, similar in design to the one in Bill's bedroom. The drawers had a few books and some magazines: National Geographic, Conde Nast Traveler, and in the bottom, a few body builder magazines. Perplexed, Sam stepped back and tried to figure what to do next.

Suitcases, briefcases, the chest. All the sports equipment would be upstairs, he guessed. Sam leaned his right hand against the chest and was running his left hand through his hair, confused.

Suddenly, he stiffened. Was that a noise? He pushed himself quickly around to the left.

The chest slid away from the wall, and there appeared to be something behind it on the wall. But in the same instant, Sam knew he had to go find out what he'd heard. Quickly, he slipped from the closet, turning off the light.

Excitedly, Sam crept up the hall and peered into the living room. Bill was right where he had been. Nothing seemed out of order; the front door was still locked and chained and the kitchen seemed just as he'd left it. For several minutes he stood listening and heard nothing. It must have been some noise out at the street. He decided to return to the closet.

As he started into the closet, he paused. There was something else. Something about the wall. Sam walked back to the door of the office and peered toward the end of the hall where stood a small table with a vase with a mirror over it. Hmm, he thought, and went back to the closet.

Yes, that's what he'd noticed. Though the closet seemed

to span the end of the room, its inside dimensions showed it could not possibly reach to the hall. Without hesitation, Sam pushed the chest and it easily swung away from the back wall.

Behind the chest was a dim rectangular outline, like a frame, almost the size of the chest. There were two lock screws at the top and two at each side. Sam extracted a quarter from his pocket and fit it to a screwhead. Soon he had all six screws loose. However, the panel was snugly fit. He would have to find something to pry it loose. He thought first of his knife, but the letter opener in the desk would be better. He didn't want to break the blade of his knife.

He pried along the top edge and the panel pulled away with a slight swoosh, like the sound of a plastic strip being peeled off a vacuum-sealed package. Behind the panel was a door of solid-looking wood, with a deadbolt lock on the left side. Now he would have to find the key.

Sam looked at his watch: 7:52. He hurried to the living room and started searching through Bill's pockets.

Keys, money -- a lot of money, $600 or $700. One set of keys was obviously for the BMW; Sam grabbed the other set and headed for the back closet.

Four keys but none of them fit. Back Sam went to the living room, dropping the keys on the coffee table alongside the other items. Searching through Bill's coat, Sam pulled out Bill's wallet. Credit cards, IDs. He ran his fingers inside the pockets of the soft leather, and felt something. Pulling out an inner flap, Sam removed a key. *The* key, he hoped.

Bill was still out cold, so Sam rushed back to the closet. The key fit. Sam held his breath and unlocked the door.

Lights came on automatically. Once through the 3-foot

door, Sam could easily stand. Inside was an extension of the closet, another closet the size of the first. Along the walls were cases of knives, beautiful knives and swords. Dozens. And at the far end were two items: a small filing cabinet, locked, and a safe, 2 feet wide by 2 feet deep and maybe 2 1/2 feet high, with a combination lock. Could there be weapons in the safe? Sam shook his head in defeat: he would have to get the combination from Bill, and that was not very likely right now.

He scanned the display cases of knives again and exited the secret room, locking it and pushing the chest back in place.

He wasn't sure how long before Bill would start to come around, but he had to get busy. Sam took his briefcase into the bedroom and set it on the dresser, then returned to the living room. He shook Bill and called to him, but there was no response. His pulse racing, Sam pulled Bill around and dragged him down the hall to the bedroom where he managed to get him onto the bed. Might as well make him comfortable. Besides ... Besides, what? Sam asked himself. He wasn't sure.

He removed Bill's belt and checked his pockets again to make sure they were empty. Then he opened his briefcase and pulled out the four pair of handcuffs.

Sam was very glad Bill's bed had a heavy black metal headboard and footboard. That made things easier. He cuffed Bill's wrists and ankles to the bed, fluffed up the pillows to make Bill as comfortable as he could, then stepped back and shook his head at the irony.

8:40. Now he would just have to wait. He wanted to be there when Bill awoke.

CHAPTER SEVENTEEN

Clank! Clank!

Someone was trying to break Sam's window. He jerked up with a start, trying to get his bearings, unable to find the window.

Clank!

Sam was wide awake. Quickly his mind focused on where he was, slumped on the sofa in Bill's living room. What was the sound? The bedroom. Bill's bedroom!

Gulping his heart down, Sam rushed down the hall.

"You son of a -- what the hell's going on?" Bill demanded.

"Now take it easy."

"Take it easy? What's the matter with you? Are you crazy?!"

"Now, Bill, it doesn't do any good to act so wild. You can't get loose."

"Unlock me, you idiot! I'll kill you!"

Sam stepped back, taking a deep breath. "Yeah, that's what I was afraid of."

For several moments they stared at one another while Bill boiled with anger. He jerked the cuffs again and fell back on the pillows.

Forcing himself to breathe deeply, Bill finally opened his eyes. With contrasting calm he said, "Why are you doing this, Sam?"

Sam hesitated before replying.

"Okay," he said. "I'll tell you."

Bill nodded for Sam to continue.

"I'm taking over the job, Bill."

Bill stared, then shook his head. "What job? What are you talking about?"

His heart pounding furiously, Sam took a deep breath. "The hit. On Lastretto."

He thought he saw a steely flicker in Bill's eyes, but Bill said only, "You're not making any sense."

"I was there, Bill. There on the stairs."

This time there was a noticeable twitch in Bill's eyebrows. He replied, not as calmly as before, "Stairs?"

"On the stairs at work. I was there in the alcove behind the door when you spoke with Barry about the hit. I know it was you. I recognized you."

Bill's face had gone ashen.

"I thought about it," Sam continued. "Over and over. And I decided I could do it. Part of that was stopping you."

Bill's voice cracked as he almost shouted, "Who are you?"

"Just me," said Sam calmly.

"Barry sent you. You're with one of them. What do you want?"

His eyes searching Bill's distressed face, Sam said, "Nobody sent me. I'm just me. Sam Robbins. I'm nobody. Nobody you'd know. But I know, I *know* I can do this. And, Bill, I don't want anything."

"And all this? I thought we were friends. You don't have to do this. Turn me loose, Sam."

"No. No way. This is the only way I can be sure you'll stay

put. It's better like this. I thought I might --"

"Might what? Have to kill me?"

"I am going to do the job, Bill. Or is it Will?"

Again Bill slumped, turning his face away toward the wall, his arms hanging from the wrist cuffs. "Jesus, Sam," he said barely above a whisper. "Do you know what you're saying? Do you have any idea?" He turned slowly, a pained look meeting Sam's eyes.

"I think I do."

"You think you do." With a sneer, Bill repeated, "You think you do. Okay, you heard Barry. You figured out about my --"

"Your other career."

Instead of nodding, Bill shook his head. "And you think you can just, what? Walk into -- where is it, Sam?"

"Carlo's. Tomorrow. 11:30."

Continuing to shake his head slowly, Bill said, "You really did your homework, didn't you, boy?"

Sam thrust his chin up smugly. "I'm not your 'boy,' and yes, I did."

"You're just going to walk into Carlo's Restaurant, pull out your six-shooters and start blazing away." Bill's hard stare was like a challenge.

"What difference does it make? I didn't ask how you were planning to do it."

"Go ahead. Ask."

"Okay, how? You're the professional."

With a cold laugh, Bill said, "You slay me." Then he cut his eyes back to Sam with a half sneer. "Just an expression. You're right, Sam. I didn't get all this," he motioned around the room with his eyes, "by working down at the office."

"Well, I'm not stupid. I saw your check stub."

Bill chuckled wearily. "You're a real trip, man."

"Yeah. Methodical. Careful."

"Jeez."

"How were you going to do it, Bill?"

"Well, it's like this, Sammy."

"Cut the crap, man," demanded Sam.

"Yeah, okay. You're the boss." Then Bill raised his eyebrows, sounding very matter-of-fact. "I was going to walk into Carlo's. Get a table for lunch, you know. Then when he had a nice mouthful of linguine and his goons were staring at their nails, I pull out my .22 Magnum -- with the silencer -- and let 'em have it. Whap, whap, whap."

Sam had settled his butt on the edge of the dresser. "Just like that?"

"Yeah. Simple as that. Take out the closest guard first, of course."

"Yeah," said Sam, pondering.

"Ha ha ha," Bill roared. "You don't have a clue, do you?"

Staring him straight in the eye, Sam answered, "More than a clue. I have a plan."

Bill nodded that he was waiting, so Sam added, "I use a shotgun --"

"A shotgun?! What a putz!"

"Whatever. You want to lend me your gun?"

"Up yours."

"Yeah. Well, a shotgun will do the job nicely."

"Real professional, Sam." Bill said the word dripping with sarcasm.

Sam stood and looked at his watch. It was almost 4 in the

morning. Just a few more hours.

"Look, Bill, I'm sorry but I have to go now. I've got to get things together."

"You're not going to leave me like this," said Bill indignantly.

Turning in the doorway, Sam smiled. "You'd rather I just put one in the middle of your forehead?"

Bill stared at him, angry, but unsure. Sam headed up the hall.

"Hey, Sam," Bill called, "what am I supposed to do? What if I have to pee?"

"You want me to come hold it for you? I could bring a cup," Sam said from the kitchen.

After a brief silence, he heard Bill mutter, "Go to hell."

Sam shook his head resolutely and headed for the front door.

CHAPTER EIGHTEEN

Sam reached his apartment before 5. He hadn't slept much, but he was way too wired to rest now. Besides, there wasn't really enough time.

He checked over his costume and weapons, and reviewed his plans. He would have a doctor appointment or eye checkup if anyone at the office asked why he was leaving at 10. Probably nobody would. Then he would hurry to his apartment.

His heart was pounding, but he felt confident. More confident and more alive than he'd felt in a long time.

No run today. But he would take a long walk in to work. He worried about Bill. Surely he wouldn't be able to get loose, but it was too late to do anything about it.

At 5:45 a.m., Sam headed to the shower and turned on the water. And waited. Right, he nodded, feeling the cold water. No Raul today.

Just as well, he told himself. This would get him going.

He arrived at the office at 7:20 and started right to work. He must keep busy to calm his jitters, although he found he was checking his watch every 10 or 15 minutes. At 8 he went down to the cafeteria and had a plain omelette for breakfast. Apple juice and decaf tea. He was starved, but didn't know if he could handle much.

Back upstairs. 9 o'clock finally came. He checked his work schedule and tried to muddle through one of his projects. It was not easy to keep his mind on it.

9:45. Sam looked up to see Peter, his supervisor, staring down at him.

"Where you been?" his boss asked.

"Right here," said Sam impatiently.

"Well, anyway, meeting at 10:30."

Sam's heart jumped. Then through gritted teeth, he replied, "Can't make it."

"What do you mean, can't make it?"

"Doctor's appointment. Eye exam. Couldn't get it any other time." Then, for emphasis, he added, "Sorry."

"Why didn't you say so?" Pete demanded. "This is a planning meeting."

Sam stared straight at him and said, "You never asked. I would have told you. You never said anything about a meeting. I can't make it, Peter. I'm sure you'll plan whatever you're going to with or without me."

"I really don't need this kind of attitude from you, Sam," Pete said.

Sam wanted to get up and punch him, but he clenched his hidden fists and turned to the supervisor. "Peter, I really am sorry. I'd change the appointment but it's taken me a month to get this one. And my eye keeps twitching." He allowed his left eye to twitch a few times to demonstrate.

Squinching up his own eyes, Peter said, "All right Sam. I guess it can't be helped this time. But check in with me as soon as you get back."

"Thanks, Pete," Sam answered sweetly. "Put in a good word

for me." And he turned back to his work.

Peter stood there silently for another moment, then turned and walked away. What a pain, thought Sam.

He couldn't risk another delay. Grabbing his jacket, Sam left immediately.

He was in his apartment by 10:15. The guns were already in curtain boxes and strapped on the two-wheel cart; his clothes were laid out. All he had to do was change, and he could have his makeup on in 10 minutes. Better to be ready early, though, so he charged right into it.

Everything was go by 10:40. Pulling his cart, Sam left the apartment. He decided to walk. If time got close, he could grab a cab.

He went down Broadway to Prince where he crossed over to Little Italy. On Mulberry he headed south past the Italian grocer, the souvenir shops and three or four Italian restaurants until he was at the corner just up from Carlo's. This is it, he told himself and slowed his walk to a respectable little old lady pace.

As he entered, he saw Carlo, his back toward Sam, talking and gesturing to the bartender. The large man who had been Lastretto's guard last week sat near the front door, seemingly browsing his newspaper, carefully noting the lady who had just entered pulling her shopping cart. Sam knew Lastretto was already here.

By the time Carlo was hurrying toward him, Sam had spied Lastretto at the same table as before. And the other guard, if there were only two, chatted with a woman at the kitchen door. Only three other customers were in the restaurant: an elderly couple near the front to the right of the door and a single young man at a table in the rear corner, also on the right. No one else sat at any of the tables on the left except Lastretto.

Carlo half-bowed showily. "Madame. You please us with your return. What can I do for you today?" At least twice he glanced back at Sal Lastretto, causing Sam to smile to himself. The door guard looked up and casually appraised the greeting.

"Yes, thank you," Sam answered smartly. "Just get me a quiet table in the back, please."

"Certainly," said Carlo and led him toward Lastretto.

"Young man," said the little old lady.

Carlo turned back toward her, "Yes, madame?"

"I'll just take that one over near the young gentleman," Sam said, pointing to the young guy on the right.

Carlo's quizzical look turned to a knowing grin. "Of course. Right this way."

Sam shooed Carlo away and settled himself with his back toward the kitchen wall, with Lastretto diagonally to his right. When the young man looked up, the little lady nodded a smile, then turned to the menu.

Before Sam could take a breath, Carlo was back, presenting a bottle of Chianti. Sam gave him an impatient old woman stare over his glasses and said, "Mr. Carlo. No wine. Just bring me a nice bowl of soup and some of that bread."

Carlo nodded, pausing, and Sam added, "Now run along. I'll just keep the menu and browse the desserts."

Hiding his annoyance, Carlo turned and headed to the kitchen.

Sam laid the menu down and pulled the shopping cart close to the left side of his chair. Casting a quick glance at the young man two tables away, Sam checked that he was engrossed in his paper. Then Sam carefully raised the end of the shotgun box and made sure the front panel would flip open as he'd designed it. Everything was working fine. He could grasp the shotgun butt and swing it around in a second.

The waiter came with the soup and bread while Carlo attended briefly to Lastretto. Lastretto, however, appeared somewhat annoyed at the interruption so Carlo was soon back at the bar. Everything seemed quiet. Sam wondered if this was the moment.

His heart pounding so hard it made his hands tremble, Sam reached over and lifted the top of the box holding the shotgun. He was just about to flip the front panel open when someone came through the entrance, catching not only Sam's attention but that of the two guards and Mr. Lastretto himself.

The door guard was already rising and reaching for the man in the brown-trimmed gray uniform as the kitchen guard moved into view, his hand under his jacket.

"Hold it," said the door guard.

"Oh. Package," began the man, reaching into the large bag hanging over his left shoulder. "Jesus!" he gasped as he found himself staring down the barrel of the guard's pistol.

"Take your hand out real slow," the guard commanded.

"H-hey, no problem. My god, it's just a p-package."

"Package for who?" said Carlo as he approached.

The man nervously swung his head from the gun to Carlo and back to the gun. "For uh ... Let me check."

"Uh-uh," said the guard with the gun.

"Hey, man," the man said shakily, "I just deliver packages. I can come back if this is a bad time."

Sam witnessed all this, his left hand sweating on the butt

of the shotgun. He would wait, he decided, when suddenly another man appeared at the entrance, behind the door guard. Before Sam could realize what was happening, the man whipped up a long-barreled pistol.

"Pap," said the pistol as it jumped slightly in the man's hand.

A wide look of surprise was on the door guard's face as he seemed to spring unnaturally to his left.

"Pap, pap," the pistol chirped again, and Carlo stopped in mid-stride, his mouth flung open. Then too many things were happening all at once.

As Carlo was dropping to the floor, the delivery man pulled out another long-barreled pistol from the bag. At the same time, the kitchen guard whipped out his ugly automatic while Sal Lastretto flattened himself against the wall.

"Boom!" went the blast from the guard's pistol. The sound reverberated around the room, deafening all inside, the bullet from the blast shattering the plate glass to the left of the entrance.

Each of the intruders apparently had his own specialty, for the last man in concentrated on the second guard, "Pap-pap-pap," knocking the guard against the kitchen wall while the delivery man calmly took aim at Sal Lastretto.

"Whap!" Lastretto's head bounced off the wall, a dark hole the size of a nickel appearing just above his wide eyes.

It was all so fast Sam hadn't had time to release his grip on the shotgun. But as the killers swung around to survey their work, Sam's brain kicked into gear.

The second the two assassins' eyes met in silent agreement, Sam flipped the front panel on the box and in one fluid movement, swung the shotgun out and up. Just as the closest of the killers, the delivery man, was raising his left hand to point toward Sam, Sam pulled the trigger.

The blast almost knocked him off his chair. But Sam braced himself with his right leg and pumped the shotgun and fired again. Taking no chances, he repeated -- over and over -- pump and fire, pump and fire, until he'd emptied five shells.

His breath coming in quick gasps, just short of sobs, Sam kicked the chair aside and stood up, another shell already pumped into the chamber. The resounding roar bouncing off the walls almost made him dizzy, but Sam forced himself to take stock of the situation.

Both killers lay piled near the door guard; just to the right, Carlo was sprawled face down. The kitchen guard sat slumped against the kitchen wall, his chin on his chest, a trail of blood smeared down the wall from where he'd stood. And Sal Lastretto still sat wide-eyed in his chair, as though the hole in his forehead had a nail holding him to the wall.

Sam's ears had begun a loud ringing, or more like a steady squeal, and his head was pounding, but he was picking up other sounds. The elderly man and woman lay whimpering in one another's arms near the back wall, the woman's stockings torn and her skirt rumpled around her waist. The young man hadn't moved. For a moment, Sam thought he'd been shot but could see his arms shaking as they covered his face.

It couldn't have been much time, but Sam realized he had to leave. Now. He snapped the shotgun back into its hiding place, grabbed the cart and started for the entrance.

Mid-room he stopped. And, like it was a well-honed instinct, Sam flipped out his green-handled C25 knife and took a step toward Lastretto. Indeed he had rehearsed this. He'd planned to draw the blade across the throat of Sal Lastretto, his own personal signature. But the bitter taste rising in his throat stopped him in his tracks. No, there had already been enough. Better to get out of here before he threw up.

Slipping the knife back into his pocket, Sam grasped the cart and hurried out the door, suddenly remembering to behave like the old woman, shouting, "Oh my. Oh my," as he hobbled up the sidewalk which was packed with people rushing toward Carlo's Restaurant.

His watch said 11:50. He'd been gone from work since 10, so he knew he needed to get back. But wait. Bill. He couldn't just … he had to go there before going back to the office.

Sam dared not take a taxi. And besides, it wasn't that far to his apartment. If he hurried.

He hoped his little old lady didn't walk too much out of character, but he made it back home by 12:15. He stashed the cart with the weapons, stripped out of the costume and jumped in the shower. It was as fast as anything. Just a few minutes, he thought. To let the bizarre scene drain away.

Hurriedly, he put his work clothes back on and ran out the door. As an afterthought, just before he closed the door, Sam went back and rummaged through a drawer in the kitchen and came up with a pair of disposable dark glasses, the ones he'd got when he had his eyes dilated last year. This would help when he went back to work.

Sam ran directly to the subway stop on Broadway. It would be the fastest way to get uptown. He just hoped he wouldn't have to wait long. Already it was past 12:30. Up and down the platform he paced, trying to make the train hurry, starting to relive the events at Carlo's in his mind. He'd done it. By god, he'd done it!

As he boarded the train, he found himself wondering, Why don't I feel better? And besides, he hadn't really done it. As the train lurched forward, Sam dropped into a seat and stared out the windows to the darkness of the tunnel.

At 86th Sam hurried from the train and ran up the stairs. He had begun to worry about Bill. Was he all right? He couldn't help it. Still, he forced himself to a walk and tried to blend in with the pedestrian traffic.

At 83rd, it was difficult to keep from running. But he maintained his grip. There was Bill's building just half a block ahead.

A short distance from the door, something clicked in Sam's mind. There was a car across the street. It had been parked there in the early morning when he'd left. And he was sure there'd been a man sitting in it. Panic rushed through his limbs.

Wait a minute! he commanded, stopping under a blossoming dogwood tree. Just calm down. This is New York; alternate side parking. The guy was probably just waiting until the right time, having just moved his car, so he could go back and get some sleep.

Yeah. Okay, he nodded, and walked up the steps to Bill's door.

He fished out the key he'd taken from Bill and -- the door was open. Just slightly, but definitely open. Sam stood frozen and listened.

He heard nothing. He looked both left and right but saw no one. Biting his lip, he slipped on the surgical gloves, put his hand on the knob and slowly pushed the door open.

There was silence inside as he walked through the entrance hall and into the living room. Nothing seemed out of place since this morning. Then how had the front door? Surely he hadn't left it open like that. Wait! Voices. Or a voice, at least. The bedroom?

Sam spied the empty Scotch bottle on the counter and carefully picked it up and crept down the hall. The voice grew louder. Just outside the door to the bedroom, he stopped.

"... don't know how you did it, but you made it real easy for me."

"Rot in hell, you slime," said Bill.

Sam's head snapped up. What?

Pap! barked the man's pistol. Sam whirled through the doorway, the bottle raised high. There stood a man in a long black raincoat, turning toward him with a startled look.

Crash! Sam cracked him across the left side of his forehead, breaking the bottle, and the man went down. For a second, Sam stood holding the neck of the bottle, looking down at him. The man did not move. Sam quickly retrieved the man's gun. Only then did he finally look at Bill.

Bill strained against the handcuffs at his wrists, his eyes clenched tightly closed. Blood soaked the left side of his shirt.

"Oh, Jesus," cried Sam, running to the bed. He fumbled in his pocket to find the key and unlocked Bill's left hand. Bill immediately gripped his chest. Sam leapt to the other side and unlocked the right hand and then hurried to unlock his legs.

"God, Bill. What! Oh my god!" said Sam.

"Sam ... ah, damn."

"Let me see. It's -- I'll call a doctor. I'll call 911," Sam said, jumping from the bed.

"No," said Bill, still choking off his words, "finish him."

"What?"

"Rosano. Finish him. He'll kill us both."

"I," Sam uttered, standing with the gun with the silencer on it. "Just --"

"Shoot him!" Bill shouted with a grunt.

Pap! Pap, pap, pap! Sam fired into the man's head and body. The body jumped with each shot.

Sam stood trembling. There was absolute silence broken by a gasp from Bill. When Sam turned toward him, Bill was rolled up on his right side, clenching his chest.

"Bill! Jeez!" Sam ran to the other side of the bed and grabbed the phone.

"Leave it," grunted Bill.

"But --"

"Leave it," Bill repeated with a long sigh. "It's no use."

"Bill, I'm sorry. I didn't know."

"You didn't know anything, you dope."

"But I just wanted to make the hit. Oh god, I'm sorry, Bill. I didn't mean for," Sam's voiced quavered, tears filling his eyes.

"Sam," said Bill, opening his eyes, "what happened?"

"I went there. To Carlo's. Two men came in and shot Lastretto and his guards. And Carlo. I think they were going to kill us all. I pulled out the shotgun and I killed them."

"You --" Bill sort of choked and laughed at the same time. "You killed them?"

"I had to."

"Ha," cough-cough. "That must have been a big surprise to them." Bill grimaced, tried to push himself up and then clenched his eyes in pain.

"Bill. Let me help. God, let me call the --"

Bill waved him off and said, "You all right, man?"

Surprised, Sam said, "Yeah. I'm fine."

"That's good. I can't believe you. You're a crazy son of a -- ugh."

"Bill," Sam pleaded as he picked up the phone.

"Forget it, Sam. It won't help." Bill breathed in and let out a long sigh. "Listen, man." He gripped Sam's shirt and pulled him close.

"I thought maybe you were right," he continued. "I lay here figuring you probably kept me from getting killed."

"But I got you shot. Having you locked up like that."

"You were right, Sam. I would have killed you. And this scum would have killed me anyway. He's one of Barry's."

"Barry? The guy on the stairs?"

"The lowest of the low, that guy. I should have guessed it was a double-cross."

"Barry sent this guy?"

"Rosano. Yeah." Bill grimaced, lay his head back a second. "Forget all that. You got to get out of here."

"I can't just --"

"Yes you can. Look, Sam, go to the dresser. Go on."

Sam paused, then rose and walked over to the dresser, stepping over Rosano's body.

"Open the drawer on the left. Top one. Ugh," he grunted, "Yeah. Now the ... shelf with the cuff links and rings."

"This?" Sam asked.

"That's it. Grab the center and pull it up."

Sam did.

"Lift the tab."

Sam pulled up the small tab at the center of the tray. Underneath were two keys.

"Now listen carefully. There's a closet in the other room. Behind the dresser in there."

"I found the hidden room," Sam told him. "I got the key from your wallet."

With a chuckle that seemed more like a grimace, Bill said, "Good. The silver key, there's a safe."

"In the corner of the room, yeah," Sam said.

"Um, uh. The combination is 12, 22, 43. Left, right, left. That's left 12, two turns right to 22 and left to 43. Got it?"

"I got it, Bill. Now let me call an ambulance."

"Shh. Listen," Bill said weakly. He coughed twice, the second one bringing a dribble of blood to his lips. "Sam, I got nobody. There was my mother, but ... And you, you tried to be a friend. Or maybe you didn't."

"No, really, Bill. I do like you. I like you a lot."

"Me, too," Bill said with a painful smile. Then, "There's not much time. There's a box in the safe. Use the silver key. No, don't argue. No time."

"The other key, gold one, listen. A house I have, in Queens. Key's on my keychain. Take the BMW, out the back in the garage." He was weakening fast. Sam knelt by the bed and Bill gripped his hand.

"The house," Bill breathed. Sam leaned close as Bill whispered the address.

"There's a big wall," Bill continued in a raspy voice. "P-panel, behind a mural. You'll find it. Behind the panel ... gold key goes in the lock. You'll see."

"Okay, Bill. Please."

"S'okay. It's all okay now." And he relaxed.

"Oh, no. Bill."

"Sam," he whispered hoarsely.

"Yes," said Sam, frightened.

"Take it. Take it and go."

"I --"

"And fing-fingerprints. Wipe 'em here."

"Okay, Bill. I'll --"

"Sam?"

"Sure, Bill. I'm here." He gripped a little tighter, trying to hold on to his friend.

"Barry."

"What?" said Sam, leaning closer.

"Get Barry. For me. He set ... set this all up."

"Barry? He did this."

"Rosano ... Barry. Get 'im for me. Ugh ... uh ... Get 'im."

"I will, Bill. I'll kill that scum."

His breath labored, Bill clenched his eyes and shook his head. "No, Sam. Wrong. It's wrong. My mother was right. I see her telling me now. Forget it, Sam. She's telling you, take the money and get out. Barry ain't worth it. Get away from this life. Get away." And he relaxed, loosening his grip on Sam's hand.

Sam sat staring, still holding tightly. He pulled Bill's limp hand, then laid it on Bill's chest. Swallowing hard, he reached and felt alongside Bill's neck. No pulse. He tried again in two more places. Nothing.

With a deep, releasing sigh, Sam rocked back on his heels, holding his left hand to his mouth a minute. Then he covered his eyes, slowly massaging his temples. Another sigh.

"Damn. I am so sorry, man. So sorry."

He stared at Bill's inert body, then backed away and noticed the body of Rosano on the floor, as if for the first time. "Barry," he said.

Sam opened his right hand and looked at the two keys. His gaze turned to the gun on the bed as he became aware of the smell of gunpowder. As he stared in the mirror over the dresser, Bill's words suddenly clicked in. Fingerprints. Get Barry.

"Fingerprints," Sam repeated. He walked to the doorway to the hall and started to think. What had he touched in the times he'd been here? It was not easy to quell his feeling of panic.

Sam reached in his inner coat pocket, found the keys for the handcuffs and unlocked the four sets of cuffs from Bill's bed and slipped them in his pocket. The gun, he'd take it. No, not good. It had killed Bill. But it had also killed Rosano. Sam picked it up, put the safety on and stuck the gun in his belt. Then he pulled the silk handkerchief from Rosano's breast pocket and started through the house.

The bathroom. Sam wiped every surface he could have possibly touched in his visits. Then he moved to the living room and kitchen, first locking and chaining the front door. He tried to remember every place he might have touched and wiped it. The glasses were all clean except for last night's. And the bottle.

Damn. The other bottle, the one he'd broken over Rosano's head. He'd have to get what was left. And all the pieces.

Twenty minutes of going over the downstairs and Sam headed upstairs to the gym. He found the basketball and wiped it, even checked spots on the floor. And on the way out, he wiped the light switches and the door.

Back downstairs, he went over it all again. He thought he had everything. Sam took a deep breath and, without looking into Bill's bedroom, headed to the back room again.

Inside the hidden room, he went directly to the safe and opened it, wondering what he'd find. Special guns? Jewels? Inside the safe was a box, 2 by 2 feet and a foot deep. He put the silver key in and lifted the lid. Inside was cash. Lots of cash. Stacks and stacks of $100 bills. Sam couldn't guess how much it was. More than he'd ever seen in his life.

He set the box on the floor and examined the rest of the safe. There were insurance papers, investment information, and some jewelry. Sam decided to leave it and closed the door. He took the box and left the room, closing everything up.

In the living room, he went over everything in his mind again. He thought he got it all. He hoped so. He got the keys to the BMW and headed down the hall. At the bedroom he choked back his feelings as he stared at Bill. Biting his lip, he walked over and put the gun back in Rosano's hand. Then he left through the back.

As he got in the car he looked at his watch: 2 o'clock and -- oh my god! Work! He had to get back.

After a moment's panic, Sam calmed himself. Okay, okay. He could call in and tell them he wouldn't be back. No. Better he should go back. Be calm. Act like nothing had happened. But what about the BMW? He decided to drive down and park it in one of the lots on West Broadway. Then he could pick it up after work and, well, he would see then.

CHAPTER NINETEEN

A million things zipped through his mind as Sam drove downtown. What had happened at Carlo's after he'd left? Had anyone, Barry's people or the police, found what had happened at Bill's? It didn't matter, he couldn't go back. Maybe he should have burned the place. No, no reason to involve a lot of innocent neighbors. And Bill ... Sam swallowed hard. Damn! He'd never intended for it to end up like that.

After parking the BMW, Sam hurried to work. He put on the throwaway shades before he entered the building, and was back at his desk by 2:30. He would stay late. It would take him hours to calm down anyway.

For a long time he just stared at his computer screen. His head was in such a swirl, everything seemed surreal. His hands had stopped shaking, but after what they had done, they appeared almost alien as he examined them. Bill ... his friend. What had he done? he asked himself, staring blankly.

For several minutes more he sat immobile. Shaking his head and letting out a long sigh, he looked over and saw a note from his boss, Pete.

Sorry you couldn't make the Planning Mtg. I did, as you said, put in a good word for you. Hope your eyes are doing okay. Here's looking at you.

Sam chuckled, at first to himself and then aloud. And then

he was laughing. "Hahahahaha."

His neighbor, Jack, in the next cubicle stood up and looked over the divider. "You all right, Robbins?"

Sam just said, "That Pete. He's a character," and laughed aloud again.

Jack shook his head and returned to his seat.

His depression somewhat lightened, Sam started flipping through his schedules on the computer, checking his current projects. Perhaps he could get some of the backlog cleared up before he left today. Relieved, he started digging into it.

After quite some time, or perhaps it was only a short while, Sam was interrupted by Pete's voice. "So, Sam, I see you were up to your dirty work at noon."

"What?" responded Sam, startled.

"Is your eye doctor in Little Italy?" Pete half-sneered.

"What? No. On the, uh, midtown."

"Oh," Pete continued with his big joke, "I guess that wasn't you, then."

"Wh-what do you mean?" asked Sam.

"Well, it was on the news. My wife called. Someone snuffed out Salvatore Lastretto. Channel 2 was doing an interview at a movie set a couple of blocks away and they were all over it like a swarm of ants."

Swarm of hornets, thought Sam, rolling his eyes. But before he could think he said, "No shit?"

Pete chuckled wide-eyed at such an uncharacteristic response from Sam, confirming with, "No shit. Made the feds look pretty bad. Right under their noses."

"The feds!" Sam all but gasped.

"Well, sure. You don't think they'd let their star witness go wandering around, do you? His two federal watchdogs got blown away with him."

"Jesus!" said Sam.

Pete paused with a concerned look. "Get a grip, Sam. I don't think they'll be coming in here."

Sam answered by just staring at Pete, his mouth agape.

"And," said Pete, "don't worry about the meeting. I'll fill you in tomorrow. After the word started spreading, everyone was either glued to the news or spreading rumors. Either way, not much got done, if you know what I mean."

Forcing a grin, Sam said, "Yeah. I see what you mean."

"Well, sorry I didn't get to you earlier. You better put those glasses back on and protect your pretty blue eyes, Frankie."

"Frank?" Sam frowned. "Oh, ha ha," he laughed.

Wonderfully satisfied with himself, Pete turned and walked away. Sam even forgot to remind himself what a jerk Pete was.

Since it was a quarter after 5, Sam decided, what the hell. He was going to get out of there before something else came up. As he stood and gathered his things, he saw Pete passing by, carrying his briefcase.

"See you tomorrow," said Pete. Then he leaned closely, confiding, "Want to get on home and get all the juice on the news."

"Sure thing," Sam replied.

Pete waved, heading for the door. Sam took his time getting his things together, made a stop in the bathroom, all to give Pete plenty of time to get away from the office. Soon Sam was striding up the street toward the parking lot.

He worried about being in the BMW, but decided to risk it, convincing himself that time was on his side. He drove up

FDR Drive, crossed the East River via the Williamsburg Bridge and swung onto the Brooklyn-Queens Expressway. Driving north, Sam reviewed the notes he had made after consulting a map back at his desk. Half an hour later he turned east on Grand Central Parkway. He passed LaGuardia airport, heading toward the Whitestone Bridge. Just before it, Sam made a quick exit and turned right onto Third Avenue. A few blocks later he found the street and turned again.

One, two blocks, and there was the house, set back in the trees. He drove on past, casing the area. There was no traffic and he didn't see anyone walking, but the houses did seem lived in. A couple of blocks later, Sam turned around and headed back to Bill's place.

He pulled into the driveway, past the huge trees, and parked next to the house. He could hear the traffic on the expressway a couple of miles away.

The day was beautiful, 65 and sunny with a few fluffy clouds. It smelled so clean and perfect, Sam began feeling suspicious and jittery. He half wished he'd brought along Rosano's gun.

Looking both ways as casually as possible, Sam walked up to the door and tried a couple of the keys on the key ring until the door unlocked. He stepped inside an almost stark room with highly polished hardwood floors and only a couple of high-backed white wood chairs on either side of a black oriental table. Sam locked the door and walked on into the next room, a more or less empty dining room, where a few carefully stacked boxes stood in one corner, and then to the kitchen.

The slatted blinds were only slightly opened, but the broad skylight let in plenty of light. Sam looked in the refrigerator. It was well stocked with soda and imported beer. There was also some cheese and condiments. Not much else. He walked into a hallway and turned left and stopped at the first doorway. There it was. A large mural of an early Thanksgiving scene covered most of the wall between this and the next room.

A daybed sat before a long, almost ceiling-to-floor window. Sam put one knee on it and leaned across and opened the blinds. The mural was quite striking, the colors vibrant. And somewhere within it ...

He began to examine the wall carefully, trying to find a handle or insert. First he went around the edges, then scanned the whole mural. Then he saw it. Near the center was a cart filled with autumn harvest. The back of the cart had a handhold, which, with the lifelike quality of the mural, could easily be overlooked as a part of the painting. Sam slipped his fingers into the slot. And then noticed a similar one to the left at the edge of a tree.

He tried to slide or pull the slot on the right and nothing happened. But trying both slots at once, he found the mural separated into panels and slid apart about 4 feet. Sure enough, there was a door, flush in the wall. The gold key fit into the lock and Sam pushed the door open.

Lights came on immediately as he stepped into a windowless room about 6 feet across and as wide as the first room. Probably 14 feet. The walls were covered with swords, knives and guns, many of them ancient looking. In one section on the right end, however, the guns were modern and arranged in a much more accessible manner. Shelves below them housed boxes of ammunition, clips, silencers and other accessories. Sam was in awe.

He thrilled to the touch of the weapons, even though he wore the surgical gloves. There were deep blue, polished chrome and black automatics and revolvers. And at the far end were a couple of red plastic-looking ones. Curious, he picked one up. The barrel had no opening in the bore and the gun was solid plastic having the shape and heft of a real gun. A training pistol? he wondered. He set it back in its place.

At the right end of the room was a large map of New York City with a few pins stuck in it. On wide shelves below the map were several other maps. And below the shelves was a squat cabinet with two drawers. Sam pulled out the top one. In the front was a folder; the rest of the drawer contained only a small cardboard box. The folder itself was actually a three-ring binder, securing maybe 50 pages. On the first page was the name Barry Rabinowitz followed by a phone number. Below this was "Hm," followed by another phone number and an address.

The following pages had other names, numbers and addresses, about 20 or 25 pages worth. The rest of the pages were blank. Sam put the folder back in the drawer and slipped the lid off the box. It was filled with matchbook covers, carefully arranged, from restaurants and bars around the country. And a few from Europe, particularly Switzerland. He looked at them a moment, wondering, and then slid the lid back on and closed the drawer.

In the bottom drawer was a long metal box, like a safety deposit box. Sam removed it from the drawer and set it on the floor. Sure enough, it had a lock. Searching through the keys on Bill's key ring, Sam came up with a small key that fit. The box, like the one from Bill's place in the city, was stuffed with

$100 bills. Between this box and the other one there must be ...
He picked one stack of bills from the front and counted.

A hundred bills in the stack, two stacks to a row, seven
rows. If they were all the same, that was ... $10,000 to a stack,
$20,000 to a row. $140,000! With the other box, there must
be almost $300,000!

No wonder Bill could live where he did and drive a BMW
M5. Sam noticed a card taped to the inside of the lid of the
money box. When he pulled it loose, a key dropped onto a
stack of hundreds. The card had a seven-digit number on it
with the words "Intl Bank Bahamas." Sam could only guess at
what this meant. He taped the card and the key back to the lid.

Now what? Two metal boxes of cash, rows of weapons.
Who knew about this house, anyway? Only Bill? That's what
Bill had indicated. The truth was, he was afraid to leave the
money here, but he was afraid to take it with him, too. What
would he do with it? Dig a hole and bury it? Carry it around in
a shopping bag? What was he going to do?

Sam sat on the floor leaning against the wall that adjoined
the mural, staring up at the knives and guns. He let his mind
wander back over the past few days, weeks. Will and Barry on
the stairs. Dead, they'd said. Then meeting Bill. And getting
to know him. Really getting to know him. And, damn it, he
liked the guy. Why did he have to ...? They could have been in
it together.

You're dreaming, he told himself. Bill said it: he would have
killed you. And you knew that. That's why you had to lock him
up.

But it didn't matter now. And Bill, who had been doing
this kind of work for so long, had told him to get out. Get

away from it. Thinking of the bodies in Carlo's, and Bill, and Rosano, he knew Bill was right. Or Bill's mother. What kind of life could he have, anyway?

Staring at the flat white floor, Sam tried to accept the truth. Take the money, get out and forget about it. Forget about it, he nodded, getting to his feet.

At the doorway, Sam turned and looked over all the items on the wall again, down to the modern guns and the filing cabinet. He walked out and locked the door and replaced the mural panels. Carrying the cash box, he locked the house, got in the BMW and left.

CHAPTER TWENTY

B ack in Manhattan, Sam parked Bill's BMW in a 24-hour parking lot and took the subway home. He had found some supermarket bags at the house in Queens, so he was able to carry the cash boxes without being so conspicuous. He just looked like another slob with his late night shopping.

With the traffic, he didn't get home till almost 9. He was more tired than he'd been in a long time, but he switched on the TV to see if he could catch any news about the day's events. Channel 2, Pete had said. Sam flipped the channels.

Some inane show was ending as Sam checked his watch again. "Coming up on News at 11, Mafia shootout in Little Italy with a little old lady to the rescue? Stay tuned."

He was wide awake now. And suddenly realized he was starving. Sam stood in the middle of the room thinking, barely hearing the blaring from the TV. He would have to stash the cash. Where? Sam speculated for a few minutes and decided what to do.

He pulled the mattress off his bed and raised the box springs. Yep, this would do. Sam took his C25 Clipit and slit the cheap tacking covering the bottom of the box spring, exposing the springs. First he took out $500 and then pushed the boxes into spaces between springs. In one of his boxes in the closet, he found some brown sealing tape and used it to secure the tear. The box springs and mattress back in place, Sam remade his bed. He hoped it would work.

Now he could get something to eat and wait for the 11 o'clock news.

As he started into the bathroom, his phone began ringing. What now? he wondered.

"Hello."

"Samuel. You're never there."

"I have a life, Mother," Sam said.

"Such awful things happening in the city. You should move back home."

"Really? Like what?" He couldn't resist egging her on.

"That awful shooting in downtown."

"You mean, in Little Italy?"

"Yes," she agreed. "That's the one."

"Mom, it's not downtown. It was Mafia shooting Mafia. They're not coming to the office to get me."

"Federal agents, Sam. No one's safe."

"Not even out on Long Island," he said ominously.

"This is no call for making jokes, Samuel."

"Well, okay, I'm sorry."

"When are you coming home, Samuel?"

"Mom, I have to work tomorrow."

"Yes, yes. But what about this weekend?"

"Well, I'll have to think about it. I'll see what my schedule is like."

"Your schedule," she said, like it was a lead weight around his neck. "Everyone in the city has a schedule."

Sam paused, shaking his head. "It's a part of life, Mom.

People have things they have to do. You remember, don't you?"

"I always had time for my family," she stated firmly.

"Let's not start, Mom. Not tonight. I am really too tired."

"All right, Samuel. Do consider it though. We could have a nice dinner on Sunday. After you had a good night's rest in your old room Saturday night. You could sleep late and --"

"Okay, Mother. I'll see how it works out. Now let me get my supper and I'll call you Friday."

"Dinner at 10 o'clock? People in the city."

"Mother. Please. I'll call you. Now good night."

"Samuel? All right, good night. And, do get some rest."

"I will. G'night." Sam hung up the phone with a shrug. Never mind going out, he conceded, and headed for the refrigerator.

He found some carrots and celery still in pretty good shape. Fine. It didn't take much preparation. From the cupboard he got a box of crackers and set it all on the table next to the dowdy old chair in the living room. He even treated himself to a beer. He could certainly use one.

Sam turned the sound down on the TV, settled into the chair and tore into the food. The carrots and celery were gone in no time so he filled up on crackers. A glance at his watch told him it was 9:55. He leaned his head back a second and closed his eyes, letting some of the day drain away.

A moment later he was startled by a cold wind chilling his legs. Opening his eyes, he realized he was holding the beer bottle between his thighs. He had drifted off to sleep. From the TV he could hear "and here's Jack with what's happening with the Knicks."

Knicks? wondered Sam still half-dazed. "Damn!" he swore, glaring at his watch: 11:20. "Missed the -- damn!"

Angrily, he jumped up and slammed off the TV, knocking the beer to the floor. He quickly uprighted the bottle, avoiding spilling it all. But he still had a foaming mess on his carpet. Sam stood clenching his fists and glaring at the ceiling.

"Okay." He got a towel and put it on the puddle, then sat back and drank the rest of the beer. Finally, he turned the TV back on.

"Reaction still coming in on the shooting in Manhattan's Little Italy section. Here's an interesting take: the day was saved by a little old lady. For the story we go to Jane Wilson. Jane?"

"That's right, Bill. We talked with a waiter at Carlo's Restaurant about what happened."

The waiter that Sam had seen at Carlo's appeared on the screen. "Yeah, she was in here a week or so ago. She gave the boss hell."

"Gave *him* hell?" demanded Sam.

"He's waiting on her today, even, but she sends him away. Few minutes later, these clowns come in blastin'. Poor Carlo."

"And the lady?" prompted the interviewer.

"Well, people are runnin' every which way. Tryin' to get out of the way. And out of nowhere, that lady, she's standing there with this shotgun, blastin' the goons."

"You mean, she shot the killers?"

"That's right."

"You could see all this?"

"Well, I peeked around the bar just before she cut loose."

"And then?"

"Hell, I jumped back under the bar."

"So, you never saw her actually pick up the shotgun. She was just there with it? And did you see what happened, where she went after the shooting?"

"No, ma'am! I wasn't coming out for anything. I mean, after the smoke cleared and the blasting stopped. But she was just gone."

"Like?"

"Gone. Like Batman."

"Batman?" chuckled the TV reporter. "Or Bat-gran?"

"Whatever you want to call her. She mowed those guys down and split."

The screen was filled with Jane Wilson's face again. "That's the story. Somewhere out there is a gun-toting granny, who apparently doesn't take any stuff off the bad guys."

"Thanks, Jane," the news anchor said. "Repeating our earlier story, the bad guys Jane referred to were apparently two mob hitmen who came into Carlo's Restaurant around noon today and gunned down mob informant Salvatore Lastretto and two federal agents who were guarding him. As well as Carlo Vitole, the owner of Carlo's Restaurant."

"11:30," said Sam. He closed his eyes and let out a long breath. Well, he would read about it tomorrow. Again he switched off the TV.

CHAPTER TWENTY-ONE

Sam was absolutely beat when the radio came on at 6:30, but it was Friday and he did have to go to work. He was almost ready to blow off the run, but he needed it. Really needed it. He was out the door in 10 minutes before he had time to back out.

A 40-minute run and a quick hot shower. Raul must have been up early today!

Sam didn't make it in to work until 8, so he didn't have his normal morning quiet period at the office. Several people were there already, including Pete.

For the first time in weeks Sam became engrossed in his projects. Some of the nagging problems began to clear and he made a good start on correcting several building space issues that had seemed unresolvable. Before he knew it, it was past noon.

Sam pushed back from his desk and stretched. Standing and looking across the tops of the cubicles, he could just see out the windows several rows away. It was bright and clear, so he closed his computer files and left for a walk.

It was wonderful outside. He felt exhilarated. Bustling crowds didn't even bother him, but he did head away from the heavier clumps of shoppers along Broadway.

Sam started walking, no particular place in mind. He was

just breathing the crisp air, smelling the blossoms, taking in the colors of the blooms on the trees and all the flowers before City Hall. Yesterday seemed far away.

After he passed Police Plaza and the courthouse, he realized he was following a familiar route toward Little Italy. Yesterday came back in a rush.

For a moment he was repelled, reeling. But then the fascination filled him. He was pleased at his success. And yes, there was excitement, a great deal of excitement, as he relived those minutes of battle. He was able to put off recalling his final encounter with Bill. For now, he was drawn back to Mulberry Street.

As he wound through the crowds at the edge of Chinatown, past the bins of fresh fish and exotic vegetables and Asian goods and trinkets, a police car creeping through the intersection at Canal Street brought a sobering phrase to him: the criminal returning to the scene of the crime.

Sam stopped, stunned by what he was doing. He browsed the array of items stacked on temporary shelves on the sidewalk before a small shop: a cheap metal stool, bamboo canes, toys in little red boxes covered with blue Chinese characters. Okay, he told himself. You're awake now. Just be very careful. And alert. He turned and continued.

As he waited for the light at Canal Street, he tried to appear relaxed, but he couldn't help straining to look past the traffic toward Carlo's Restaurant two blocks away. The light changed, and he moved along with the other pedestrians.

Tourists and locals were out in force. Since it was well past noon, the sidewalk tables along Mulberry were filling up with customers eager to partake of the Italian cuisine and passing scenery. Sam noted, as he always did, the delicacies in the windows. And, as always, he was pleased at the variety of languages he overheard.

Finally, he was there. Across the street from Carlo's. And he wasn't the only one drawn to this particular location. Groups of people milled around, kept at a distance by the yellow plastic police tape cordoning off the area.

"Quite a show, wasn't it?"

Sam turned to see a uniformed beat cop next to him, looking across the street.

"Wha-what do you mean?" Sam stammered.

"The mob shooting," answered the policeman.

"Oh. At the restaurant over there."

"I assumed that's what you were looking at," the cop said.

"Well, yeah. I was out for a walk and can see something's going on."

"You didn't know about it?"

"Yeah, I heard something on the news. And people at work were talking," Sam replied, as casually as he could.

The cop seemed about to walk away, but he said, "Bad news for the feds."

Sam waited a second and replied, "You mean the federal agents, the guards of uh ..."

"Lastretto. Sal Lastretto. Ready to sing like a bird. But I guess he's got too many air holes now."

Sam's face screwed up into a frown, prompting the policeman to say, "Sorry. Goes with the job," he shrugged.

"You were in there with the investigation?" asked Sam.

"Me? Nope. They aren't gonna let me in any more than you. But you want me to go over and ask?"

His heart jumped a beat, but Sam replied, "Naah. What's to find out?"

Nodding agreeably, the cop said, "Yeah, you're right there. Channel 2 and the other reporters already nailed down 'bout everything. Channel 2 was there before Homicide made it."

With a half smirk, Sam said, "Bad news for Homicide, too, then."

The cop laughed. "You got it."

Sam waved as he walked away. "Good luck with the investigation."

"Yeah, right?" said the cop, in that New York way of making the phrase into a question.

Sam walked on, forcing himself not to turn around. The cop was right, though. He needed to get a newspaper. Well, back to the office. He'd get the paper tonight.

By 3:30 Sam was heading up West Broadway, trying to figure what to do about Bill's house in Queens, about his car. Would the police be looking for it? Had anyone found what had happened with Bill and Rosano? He chewed at his lip, trying to settle the shootings at Bill's place in his mind. This was more difficult to set at ease than the events at Carlo's.

He hadn't known they were federal agents with Lastretto, of course. Besides, he didn't shoot them. He shot the bad guys. But he had gone there to kill Lastretto. Could he have done it? And if he had, he would have had to shoot the guards as well. Perhaps it was all the same.

Sam grabbed a couple of papers, went to his apartment and turned on the TV. As he dropped the papers on the table in the living room, he suddenly felt very tired. He would rest just a little, he thought. Turning the TV down to a murmur, he sank into the chair. What had he gotten himself into?

The policeman he had seen in Little Italy at lunch was opening Sam's door, startling Sam up from his chair. What was going on? The uniformed policeman pointed and in came the two federal agents. One had a bullet hole in his head, the other had two blood-stained spots on his shirt. There were police cars everywhere downstairs, with their sirens blaring. Only they sounded more like bells. Ring, ring! Ring, ring. Ring!

Sam jerked himself awake. His phone was ringing. Gasping his heartbeat back to normal, Sam struggled to his feet and wobbled to the phone.

"H'lo," he managed.

A pause, then, "Samuel. Where have you been?"

"I just walked in, Mother."

"Just walked in? It's almost 7:30."

For some reason, Sam was finding this very irritating. "Okay," he snapped, "so it's almost 7:30. I just walked in."

"All right," she said before turning to silence. "I apologize. I'm sure you're very busy. Maybe too busy to call."

Sam sighed. She really knew how to box you in. "Right, Mother. I said I'd call. Now you beat me to it. How are you doing?"

"I'm fine, Samuel. Are you coming out tonight? Or tomorrow?"

Damn! he thought. How did he always get himself into these things. "Look, Mother, this may not be a good weekend."

"Samuel. You promised."

"No, Mother, I did not promise. But look, I'm really beat

from a very long day. Why don't I call you tomorrow? And this time, I will call."

"Is that a promise? Because it sounds a little like one."

"It's not a promise. It's a statement. I have a lot of things I have to do, but I'll call by tomorrow evening."

"All right. Should I have dinner ready?"

"Dinner?"

"Tomorrow evening," she said simply.

Clenching his jaws as he shook his head, Sam felt himself surrendering. "I'll call by ... 4:30. Will that be early enough?"

"That will be fine. Thank you, Samuel."

Sam was sure he could see her habitual look of triumph. "Okay. Good night, Mother."

"Good night, Samuel. It will be good to have you home."

Patience, he told himself as he hung the phone up gently.

7:30. He'd missed all the news again. This was a repeat of last night. Except, of course, it wasn't. It was Friday night. Friday night and --

A thrill ran through him. A new BMW M5 sat in a parking lot waiting for him. A mysterious hideaway awaited in a far corner of Queens. He didn't have to be Sam Robbins, nobody, tonight.

And he wouldn't, he told himself, slamming his palm down on the counter. Two videos fell over from the impact and Sam reached to grab them, setting them upright. For a moment, he stood transfixed. Then he smiled and picked out the "Blue Steel" video and pushed it into the VCR. Nodding with approval, he turned the sound up so he could just hear it and went into the bathroom and turned on the shower. As the water got hot and steam began to slip through the doorway, Sam slowly took off his clothes as he watched the movie and swayed.

When the scene of the shootout in the deli came on, Sam watched intently as the stockbroker stood anxiously looking at the gun, finally bending and picking it up.

"Putz," Sam said. He chuckled, turning away from the TV and stepping into the shower.

Sam found himself singing. In the shower. Why had he been tiptoeing around so carefully? He wasn't like that. He had done the job. He had taken over The Hit and done it. Or would have if those idiots hadn't intervened. But they got theirs.

He laid out some nice clothes. Sam couldn't dress like Bill, but he had a few classy things. He put on his dark tan pants and a light blue polo and set out his brown casual shoes. No, he would wear his new Top-Siders. And his blue blazer. It would all go pretty well with the M5.

Twenty minutes later he was on the subway going to pick up the BMW. People were still heading home from work, the poor dopes. Sam noticed he was getting some appreciative looks. He wasn't bad looking and he was in pretty good shape. It felt good to be so free.

Sam walked by the parking lot and spied the BMW. Everything looked normal. After the attendant brought the car up, he paid him, with a nice tip, and pulled out to the street. A couple of blocks later, he pulled over and parked in a brightly lit spot. With the engine idling, he opened the console box. Inside were several CDs, set in slots. Sam closed the lid and reached over and opened the glove box. There was a small flashlight, metal, expensive. He took this and the stack of pamphlets and papers.

Owner's manual, maintenance schedule, various warranties.

He laid these aside and opened a folder. Registration, insurance certificate -- wait. Sam reread the insurance card. Then he checked the registration. The car was not registered in Bill's name. It was registered to Ellen Peters. Could that be Bill's mother? He had never told Sam her name. Sam sat a minute, wondering. He put the car in gear and pulled away with a screech.

Sam had a good sense of direction. He wouldn't need a map this time. As he cruised along the BQE, he thought over what Bill had told him about his life. It wasn't much. They'd had so little time. But Bill had told him to take the things. Take the money, the car, and he told him about the house. Maybe there was more there than he'd found.

Just a little light remained in the sky when Sam exited just before the Whitestone Bridge, but by the time he reached the house a few minutes later, the big trees had already ushered in the night. Sam parked at the end of the driveway where the car would not likely be seen from the street.

He carried in the folder of papers from the car and, using the flashlight, walked straight to the room with the mural panels without turning on any lights at the front of the house. After he was in the inner room, Sam closed the door behind him. The knives sparkled invitingly from the wall.

Sam went to the file cabinet and started going through papers slowly. He found a divider marked "CAR" and another marked "HOUSE." There was also one marked "RST HM." Out of curiosity, he opened the last one first. In it were receipts for the past two years for a rest home in Queens. The cost per year was more than Sam's salary. It must be a nice place. He let the folder close and checked the other two.

On both the titles for the BMW and the house were the same name, Ellen Peters. And when Sam flipped open the rest home folder again, he saw the name. That must be Bill's mother. There were receipts in the first two folders. Both the BMW and the house had been paid for in full. Insurance papers showed they were paid up through next February.

As he had done yesterday, Sam sat on the floor with his back against the wall, staring up at the knives. It occurred to him he hadn't looked at the rest of the house. Which he felt he should do before he allowed himself to completely relax. With some effort, he pushed himself up and left the sanctuary.

In the hallway, Sam found the switch and turned on the light. A bathroom on the right, followed by a bedroom, completely empty. On the left was a second room roughly the size of the room with the mural. This room had a few chairs and a small coffee table. And a walk-in closet with a scattering of clothes and boxes. Except for a glassed-in porch across the back, that was the extent of the house. There had really been nothing to see. Sam switched off the lights and returned to the weapons room.

Something hadn't seemed quite right about the layout of the rooms, but as he sat admiring the knives, Sam decided to let it go for now. Instead, he focused on a couple of empty slots on the wall of knives. Intrigued, he got up and opened the glass doors, sliding them aside. The empty slots were about chest high and were not slots at all. They were handles. The left was stationary, decorative perhaps. But when he pulled the one on the right, a door opened from the wall. He had not even seen the outline before.

He realized now what was odd about the house. The room,

like the one at Bill's place in the city, seemed smaller than it should have been, and what he now saw explained it. Beyond the wall of weapons was an additional 2 to 3 feet he had not accounted for. There he took a step down on a sort of landing where he could see stairs to the left. As the lights were on, Sam slipped the flashlight in his pocket and walked down.

The basement was amazing. Besides some basic furnishings, metal chairs, matching couch and easy chair, TV and radio and a small refrigerator, there was a very long room with different sized tables and counters with tripods and gun rests. It was an indoor target range.

The style of the house, long and narrow like a shotgun shack, was perfect for this setup. The range ran the entire length of the house and more, seeming to extend under most of the large backyard. Sam estimated the length to be at least 100 feet. Ceilings and walls were heavily insulated and a door at the bottom of the stairs was about a foot thick, steel on both sides. No doubt the basement was soundproof.

At the back end of the range, behind the targets, were large rolls of insulation, floor to ceiling and wall to wall. And at the head of the range, by the wall before the tables, was a large glass case of rifles of various styles and barrel lengths. On a shelf in the case were silencers, designed, apparently, for the different rifles. In the bottom of the case were boxes of ammunition.

What a beautiful collection! Sam smiled as he admired the guns. He opened the case and touched each rifle lovingly. They made the two guns he had bought look crude. With exhilaration, he sealed the door at the stairs, then came back and chose the rifle with the longest barrel. He checked the caliber, found the box of cartridges and went over to the table.

This rifle was good for a great distance, he was sure. Much more than the length of this range. He couldn't resist trying it out. Sam knew enough to pick up the earplugs and headphone-like ear protectors and put them on. He raised the barrel and sighted through the scope. The quality was excellent. He could read the fine print on a roll of insulation.

He selected a silhouette target from a stack by the side wall and set it up on a 1-inch plywood stand right in front of the insulation. Back at the table, he loaded a cartridge into the chamber, raised the rifle again and sighted through the scope. He would go for a head shot.

Bam!

Even with the ear protectors, the burst was intense. Checking through the scope, Sam saw his hit was a little low on the head and left of center. Not bad. He walked down the range and checked his target. The whole left side of the head area on the plywood was blown away. This was serious firepower.

Back at the table, Sam found the silencer for this rifle and fitted it to the end of the barrel. He loaded, sighted and fired.

Snap. The sound greatly belied the power and the kick of the rifle. This time he was almost dead center on what was left of the target.

Very pleased with himself, Sam examined each rifle in turn, stroking them with great respect. He had no doubt that each was perfectly sighted and in top condition. His uncle's farm, that's where he should be testing these babies. However, the range was perfect for the pistols upstairs.

With this astonishing variety of weapons, Sam found new admiration and regard for Bill. He wondered how long Bill had been doing this. It must have been many years. Sam put the rifles away, closed the cabinet and went back upstairs.

After he shut the hidden door and slid the knife case closed, he returned to the filing cabinet. He had decided to search through everything.

Starting at the back, there were about a dozen folders on people, with names and locations. A few facts about where they went and when. At the front was a separate folder with a yellow tab across the top. There were several pages in the folder, each with a name and phone numbers, and on some, addresses. Sam recognized two of the names: Barry Rabinowitz and Joey Napoli. (Could this be the "Joey" Bill had mentioned to Barry that day on the stairs?) There were two phone numbers and two addresses for Barry. Interesting. And three phone numbers and two addresses for Joey Napoli. One of those phone numbers was underlined and "secure" was written next to it.

Many things went through Sam's mind. He knew this information would be useful.

CHAPTER TWENTY-TWO

It was 1 in the morning and Sam felt a rush. His findings were overwhelming, but it was all opening up a whole new world to him. He wanted to go and drive into the night. And it suddenly hit him. Why not? He was a couple of miles from the Whitestone Bridge and the keys to a beautiful BMW M5 were in his pocket.

In less than an hour, he was on I-95 heading for Connecticut.

Sam resisted the urge to put the accelerator down and let the M5 do what it was supposed to: speed. A radar detector was installed in the car, tempting him further, but there were too many chances involved. Anyway, just driving the car within the speed limit was pleasurable enough.

Halfway across Connecticut, he turned north. Shortly after daybreak, he pulled off to a restaurant in Greenfield, Massachusetts. He enjoyed a quiet breakfast, taking in the emerging beauty as the sun spread light across the hills. He wondered if he could stay all day.

From the restaurant, Sam drove over and filled up with gas and got a state map. He'd had enough of city expressways and interstate highways. He needed to get farther away. He was maybe a half hour from the Green Mountain National Forest in Vermont. It had to be more remote there. He headed west on State Highway 2.

The scenery was idyllic. He didn't even have to go on to Vermont. In no time he was driving through a beautiful Massachusetts state forest, so he decided to leave the highway and head down the forest road. He found a perfect little picnic area where he stopped.

The forest freshness filled his nostrils and lungs. He reveled in the silence. It was intoxicating. Nothing but the breeze and birds. Finally, his mind began to clear. For a moment, just a moment, he closed his eyes. It was the most relaxed he'd felt in such a long time.

Sunlight filtered through the trees, turning floating pollen into golden glitter. Sam gazed through half-open eyes for some time before he realized he was not dreaming. The nearby calls of birds, the breeze in the trees, the smell of the forest mixed with the fragrance of the leather inside the BMW pulled him slowly from sleep. He glanced at the clock on the dash: 7:15.

It had been only an hour or so, but he felt as if he'd been away for days, even weeks. In the back of his mind the drama of the past few days remained, but it seemed more distant, more ... settled and done. He got out and stretched, reaching as high as he could into the canopy of the forest. It was invigorating. He wanted to walk into the woods and spend the weekend, but he knew he must get back. Sam climbed into the car and drove slowly back to the state highway, turning toward New York.

CHAPTER TWENTY-THREE

M other?"

"Hello? Sam?"

"You sound a little surprised." He smiled to himself. "I said I'd call."

"Yes, but it's early."

"I wanted to catch you before you started making your rounds."

"Sounds like I'm a doctor."

"Well, I know you have busy days on Saturday. Anyway, I don't want to hold you. I should be there by 6. That okay?"

"That'll be fine, Samuel, and I'll make --"

"Whatever you make will be fine, Mom. See you then."

"Yes, Samuel. I look forward to it."

Sam rolled on into Manhattan. It should be easy to find a parking spot at a convenient lot with so many people heading out of the city. After he had the BMW securely stowed, Sam took the subway downtown to Chelsea and his apartment.

He should be tired, but he still felt energized from his respite in the forest and the drive, so he changed and went out for a long run. It was the best he'd felt in a long time.

That evening he was beginning to flag, but his spirits were still high. He wasn't even deterred by his mother's fretting.

"I worry about you in the city, Samuel."

"The pork chops were really good, Mom. And you don't need to worry. I'm fine, really."

"But the crime. Those shootings down where you work."

"Not where I work, Mom, remember. That was Little Italy. That's not where I work."

"Well, I know, but --"

"Mom, it's okay. I'm taking care of myself very well. And with my raise, I might just take that long overdue vacation."

"You got a raise?" Her eyes widened with approval.

"Well, not so much, but enough to matter."

"But how much, Samuel?"

"Now, Mom, we don't discuss those things, do we?"

Properly chastised, she replied, "I didn't mean anything."

"I know you didn't," Sam said pleasantly. "By the way, you know that TV?"

"Oh, do you want to watch something? Go right ahead. I'll get this cleaned up."

"No, Mother, I don't really want to watch something. Thought we'd just talk. And I'll clean up. You cooked after all."

"That's not --"

"Shush, now. What I meant was, you've had that old TV for a long time."

"Since the 1980s," she replied. "RCA. Good American quality."

"I thought I'd get you a new one."

"Why would you do that? It works fine."

Smiling, Sam replied, "Except for the popping that sounds like the picture's about to explode."

"It doesn't happen that often."

"Mom, it's okay if I buy you something. A new TV, and a DVD player? You could watch some of those old movies you like over at the library."

For a moment, his mother studied him. "What's going on, Samuel? You seem so ...?"

"Nice? It can happen."

"No, that's not what I meant," she protested.

"Look, Mom. I know I've been difficult, a pain for a long time. Well, it was all part of getting independent. And that wasn't easy. You didn't want to let me."

"But, Sam --"

"That's okay. But now I've made it. I'm doing all right. So let me do something for you."

She continued to stare at him, finally answering quietly, "All right."

"Fine. Maybe we can go look around next weekend. If you know where you want to go. Now let's clean up," he said before she could respond. "I have to tell you that getting to bed and sleeping late sounds real good."

On the drive back into the city in his old Camaro on Sunday, Sam reflected. He hoped he wasn't creating a problem for himself with his mother. But, he smiled, if nothing else, it certainly had thrown her off track. Maybe it would work out.

Anyway, she had been uncustomarily quiet that morning, not banging around in the kitchen like she usually did. And he appreciated the chance to sleep until 10:30. It had been a pleasant visit for a change.

Sam picked up a paper on the way back to his apartment.

Above the lurid front-page photo of some prostitute claiming a close relationship with a local politician, another headline caught his attention: Two Bodies Found / Gangland Killings.

Inside his apartment, the windows open to let in some of the cool spring air, Sam turned to page 3 for the story. The writer hinted at a Mafia-style shooting at the house on West 83rd. He'd wondered how long it would take them.

Though the police were closed-mouthed, the story suggested a tie-in with the Little Italy massacre, since a "source" had confirmed a connection between Rosano, though they hadn't mentioned him by name, and Lastretto. They didn't say what that connection was.

Sam pitched the paper aside, satisfied. He decided to spend the afternoon watching old movies on his old VCR. And going to bed early.

Chapter Twenty-Four

Monday, Sam was getting a few work chores caught up, cleaning some of the dated junk out of his files. So busily occupied, he had managed to put Thursday's events out of his mind. He was just checking his watch, wondering about a walk on the stairs, when his phone rang.

"Hey, Sam, this is Pete. Wonder if you could come over to my cube for a few minutes."

"Uh, sure, Pete. What's up?"

"Are you free right now?"

"Yeah. I'll be right over." This was curious, thought Sam. Pete almost always came and lurked around Sam's area. Oh well, whatever.

"Sam," said Pete, standing as Sam entered, "this is Detective Carter."

"Jackson," said the detective, shaking Sam's hand.

"Mr. Jackson?"

"No, it's Carter."

"But?" Sam frowned.

The detective gave him a warm smile. "Jackson Carter. You can call me Jackson."

"Okay, uh, Lieutenant," said Sam.

"It's just Detective."

"Ah." Sam decided it was time for somebody to be quiet. He looked from the detective to Pete, back to the detective.

"Anyway," Detective Jackson Carter said, "I wonder if I might ask you a few questions?"

"Well, sure. What's it about?" Sam was fairly certain his nervousness didn't show.

"Could we go somewhere? Get a cup of coffee, take a walk?"

"Well," Sam cast a look at Pete. Pete nodded an okay in his self-assured way. Sam nodded at the detective in return.

"Come on," said Detective Carter in a friendly tone. On the way down to the lobby, Carter made idle chat about what a pretty day it was, even if it was Monday. Sam was as agreeable as he could be.

"Out here." Detective Jackson Carter led Sam out of the building. Parked at the curb was his car. Sam balked.

"It's okay. Go ahead. Get in."

"What's this all about, Detective?" Sam asked suspiciously.

"Hey, you got it right that time," grinned the detective. "But really, call me Jackson."

"Yeah, okay. But ..."

"To be honest, Mr. Robbins, I don't know where to go. I'm not real familiar with this area. I thought we might just sit in the car." The man stood quite at ease, in a gray coat and trousers that didn't quite match. He went to open the passenger side door for Sam. "That all right with you?"

"All right," said Sam. He got in the car and Carter went around to the driver's side.

The detective took a few minutes settling in. Sam would have thought, it being his car and all, it wouldn't be that difficult.

"How long you work here?"

"About eight years," Sam answered.

"Yeah?" said Carter, sounding genuinely interested. "You like it?"

"Detective," Sam said to him, "could we just get to the point? What's going on?"

Detective Carter looked at him a minute, like he was weighing his approach. "Mr. Robbins, there was a shooting this weekend on the Upper West Side."

Sam frowned. "What's that got to do with me?"

With the detective's arched eyebrows, Sam knew he'd responded too quickly. He tried not to grind his teeth too hard.

Carter began again, as though he'd been confused by the interruption. Sam was quite sure that wasn't the case.

"Well, there were two men killed." He paused to allow Sam to reply. And though Sam realized it was quite natural that he would have seen the story in the papers, he kept quiet this time. Detective Carter continued, "One of the men worked here at your company."

Sam's eyes went wide. He was surprised all right, but he hoped the detective would think it natural enough. "At our company?" he pretended with great incredulity.

"Yes," said Carter looking straight at him. "His name was Bill Jackson."

Sam frowned but he said nothing.

"Do you know him?"

"I ...?" Sam seemed to search his memory.

"Uh, Mr. Robbins, you were seen with Mr. Jackson in the company cafeteria."

Now Sam was surprised. "That Bill?"

"Yes. I believe you had lunch together."

Damn, thought Sam. Carter probably knew a lot more than that.

"Well, yeah. I just met him. He was Mafia?"

"What made you say that, Mr. Robbins?"

"Well, the papers --"

"Ah, everything looks like Mafia to them," Carter said sadly, seemingly dismissing the newspaper story.

Sam said, "Well? Was it Mafia-related?"

"Well," said Carter, seeming to weigh his answer, "it appears it might be."

"God!" Sam replied, properly awed.

"Anyway," continued Detective Carter, "you knew him --"

Gasping suddenly, Sam said, "You weren't related?"

"Pardon me?" Carter was genuinely perplexed.

"Bill Jackson? That's your name."

Detective Carter stared at him. "Jackson is my first name."

"Oh," said Sam apologetically. "It was confusing."

"Yeah. I guess it is. Did you know Mr. Jackson very well?"

Pondering a moment, Sam answered, "No. Not really."

"When you say, 'not really' ..."

"I mean, we met a few times. We had lunch. By chance. There were no empty tables, and well ..."

"Yes," said Detective Carter, "go on."

"Well, I don't really know many people, Detective. Kind of shy."

Carter just nodded.

"He was a nice guy. What a terrible thing. Someone just shot them? What happened, Lieutenant?"

"It's Detective. I'll explain in a little while. Now go on with what you were saying."

"He was a nice guy. Quiet, like me, I guess. A little shy. So we talked. And we had drinks after work." Sam decided not to try to hide everything. Maybe a little information would be enough.

"Where was that?"

"What?" Obviously he was wrong.

"Where you had drinks?"

"I don't know. It was just some place he spotted after work."

"I see."

While Sam waited placidly for Detective Jackson Carter to say something else, he zipped through his mind for other things the detective might know. He was confident that the places Bill had taken him, no one would talk about.

"And did you go somewhere after that?" asked Carter.

"We had dinner at a little Chinese place up on Seventh. Near the Village. We just grabbed something quick and he had to leave."

Detective Carter indicated that begged for further explanation.

"Said he had to get home," Sam shrugged. "That was all."

"And when was this?"

"Last, no, the previous Friday, I think it was. Lieutenant, I mean, Detective, what happened?" Sam asked as earnestly as he could.

"Well, best we can tell, someone broke in and shot both of them."

"Broke in?" Sam replied with more surprise than he'd intended. "Did they live together? The papers said something about one of them being connected with Mafia and -- wait, you said it was on the Upper West Side? That's where Bill lives? I mean, with the other man?"

"A lot of questions, Mr. Robbins," Detective Carter smiled. "Yes, Upper West Side. A house. Mr. Jackson's."

"A house?" Sam asked incredulously. "Bill had a house on the Upper West Side? And he works here?"

"Appears that's true. And the other man, Tony Rosano, no, it doesn't appear he lived there. It was his gun that killed Mr. Jackson."

"Oh, my god."

"Strange thing is, Rosano was killed with the same gun. *His* gun."

"I don't understand."

"There's a lot we don't understand." The way Carter said it as he stared out through the windshield, this certainly seemed to be the truth.

Sam sat in silence, trying to figure what to say. Maybe it was best if he kept quiet. Finally, he said, "Detective Carter, this guy, Bill. I just met him a week or so ago. I barely know him. And I don't understand this. He seemed like a regular guy, you know? I mean, what was this all about? Was the other guy his ...?"

"His boyfriend?" Carter was to the point.

Sam acted a little embarrassed. "Bill didn't seem like that."

"No," said Detective Carter, with his blank stare again. "It was more like business, I expect."

Sam inclined his head, questioning.

Detective Jackson Carter leaned over and said, "Well, Mr. Robbins, it looks like maybe both of them were involved with organized crime."

"Bill?" said Sam, his tone not believing.

"You see," Carter went on, "he was on his bed, fully clothed. But it appears he'd been chained, or handcuffed, to the bed. Marks on his wrists and ankles and scratches on the headboard and footboard."

"Jesus!" Sam put a hand over his mouth. "What was going on?"

"We're not sure. Maybe he was being interrogated. But the other guy was knocked cold before he was shot. With his own gun."

"Interr--" Sam said, "maybe it was CIA. Or something."

"CIA?" Carter stopped, rolling the thought around. "That's an interesting idea."

"Well, I mean, 'interrogated'?"

For several minutes they sat in silence. Sam stared out at the buildings, the people rushing by. This was certainly not his life of a month ago. Before he met Bill.

Detective Carter shifted in his seat. "Is there anything else you can tell me? When you last saw Mr. Jackson, what was he like then?"

Sam looked at him. What should he tell the man? "Well, it was Thursday. No, Wednesday."

"That's last Wednesday?"

"Yes. He called me in the afternoon."

"At the office."

"Right. We were still at work. He said he'd see me after work and we met in the lobby. Umm," Sam rolled his eyes up, searching his memory. "We walked up the street a ways, it was a nice day. And then he said he had some things to do. Said he'd call me."

"And did he? Call, I mean?"

"Well, no. I didn't think anything of it. I mean he was probably out. But, god, I never thought ... When did it happen?"

"What's that, Mr. Robbins?"

"When was he, when was Bill killed?"

"Coroner says it was Thursday."

"You mean, he wasn't even at work Thursday?"

"Why do you say that?"

"You said Thursday," Sam replied cautiously.

"Well, I didn't say when Thursday." Carter seemed to be trying to pry into Sam's mind. "But looks like it was Thursday afternoon. So maybe he was at work. Part of the day, anyway."

"Well," Sam said, looking down pensively, "he never called." He was quiet. He knew he'd said more than enough, but he added, "And the other man? Surely somebody saw?"

"Umm, neighbors didn't see anything," Detective Carter said, either disappointed or unconvinced. "Real quiet neighborhood there. Maybe nobody wants to see anything."

"Wow. That's too bad." Then Sam was quiet.

Detective Jackson Carter waited, bouncing the information around. Sam noticed a slight rocking of his head, as though he were considering alternatives. After a silence that began to feel uncomfortable, maybe only a minute, maybe more, Detective Carter turned and looked at him.

"Can you remember anything else?"

"No," said Sam, and he looked at the detective. "It's awful. Just terrible. An average, nice guy like that."

"Yeah," Carter said. "Well, thank you very much for your information, Mr. Robbins. I'll walk you back in."

Sam started to ask the detective to let him know if they found anything, but he decided it was best to sever this connection now. He just said, "Sure."

Sam sat at his desk, glad the interview was over, but worried what Detective Jackson Carter (seemed like he ought to add "Esq." to a name like that) knew. What he knew about Sam. He stared at his computer screen for a very long time, considering possibilities. The police were probably checking with a lot of people around the office, and he was just one of them. Still ...

His gaze wandered to his watch: 4:15. Enough for one day. Sam grabbed his things and headed home.

On his way out, he checked for Detective Carter's car. It was gone. Maybe he'd gone home for the day, too. But Sam admitted he didn't know much about police work. Maybe it was time he found out.

As he walked quickly up Greenwich Street, Sam pondered the series of events since that morning on the stairs, and especially since Thursday. He had gotten himself in very deep. And even though the men he'd shot were killers themselves, he *had* killed them. And, he reminded himself, he would have shot the guards, too. The federal agents.

Bill was right. Sam really didn't know what he was doing.

Sam walked into his apartment with all this still ringing in his head. For a moment he stared at his reflection in the window. What *was* he doing?

In a flash, Sam decided.

CHAPTER TWENTY-FIVE

Sam had carefully checked as he walked home. He didn't think anyone was following him. Nevertheless, several times he peered out his window to the street below. Nothing unusual. Sam left and headed for the subway.

Just to be sure, he changed trains once.

At the lot, Sam picked up Bill's BMW, or maybe it was Sam's now, and headed for Queens. It was a little after 7.

Traffic wasn't too bad at this hour, so he made it to the house before 8. Sam pulled to the back under the trees and walked around and let himself in. He went into the secret room to the file cabinet, where he extracted the notebook. There was Barry's page, with the two telephone numbers. He had a feeling about the phone in this room, so he picked it up and dialed Barry at the home number.

"Hello?" A woman's voice answered.

"Hello, Mrs. Rabinowitz?"

"Y-yes." It was almost a question.

"Is Barry there?"

She paused and then said, "Who is this?"

Sam smiled. "Tell Barry Will wants to talk to him."

He waited a few minutes, listening to muted voices and some scooting around. He didn't mind. He was enjoying this.

"Hello." The voice was strained and curt.

"Barry?"

"Who the hell is this?"

"It's Will, Barry. Like I said."

"How'd you get this number," demanded Barry. "Who is this?"

"Shut up and listen, Barry," Sam said bluntly. There was no protest from the other end. "You can think of me as whoever you want, Barry. You can think of me as your nightmare. But you can call me Will. Sure, I know you took care of your Will. Like you take care of all your friends, Barry?"

"Now wait a minute, you --"

"I said, shut up!" Sam snapped. "Now if I've got your attention, you're still in business. You're also well aware your boys didn't make it back from their delivery at Carlo's."

"You're, you're the little old lady?"

"As sweet as can be," chuckled Sam. "So, Barry, the jobs come in, the jobs go out. I'm talking about the hit jobs, Barry." Sam fairly growled the last sentence.

Barry clearly was not prepared for this conversation. "I ... I'm not sure."

"Okay, Barry. This is just our 'initial interview,' you might call it. I'll give you a chance to get your wits together and I'll call you again. Tomorrow."

After a brief pause, Barry answered, "Uh, sure. But not here."

"I'll call you at this same number."

No response.

"And Barry, Will was a friend of mine." Sam hung up the phone.

It was exhilarating! The sense of power he felt over the

slime, Barry, made Sam flex his muscles uncontrollably. He was pacing, standing on tiptoe. It was so good. He could do this.

Sam studied the weapons on the wall. So many fine choices. He selected three with long barrels and silencers and two small compact automatics, a .40SW and a 9mm, put them in a bag along with cartridges for each and went down to the basement firing range.

Chapter Twenty-Six

The next day at the office was mostly a blur. Sam was still so charged up over his decision to continue Bill's business that even the most mundane of tasks didn't rattle him. It didn't matter. It was like he had just realized he could play with the symphony.

And fortunately the day was routine. No visits or calls from Detective Carter. Or hassles from Peter. He believed he was even working better. Goals, he smiled. People need goals to keep them focused.

At 7 o'clock Sam was sitting in the secret trophy room in the house in Queens. He had opened the notebook and was dialing Barry's home number.

"Hello!" Barry growled into the phone before the first ring had completed.

"And a pleasant good evening to you, too, Bar-ry." Sam said it like he sometimes said Pee-ter to his boss. He couldn't help the irony he found.

"What do you want?" He could almost hear Barry grinding his teeth.

"You know what I want, Mr. Rabinowitz. I want to continue the fine business relationship you had with my partner, Will."

"Will didn't have no partner."

"Hey, there's no need to continue this hostility, Barry. We're going to be friends. Or, no, I know what you do to your friends, like Will. So let's just keep it business."

"Why should --"

"I was saying," Sam cut him off, wanting to cut more than just Barry's conversation, "I like things nice and tidy. Like Will did. Of course, he warned me about you, but you're The Man, Barry. Or I could just talk it over with Joey."

Was that a gulp from Barry? There was dead silence.

"I expect, Barry, that Joey already has some suspicions about the events of last Thursday. But I don't want to mess with the chain of command. You work with me and things will go right on like before. With both of us a little wiser, though. Right, Barry?"

"Okay, whoever you are."

"Will."

"Yeah, right. Will. Okay, Will. We'll talk."

"That's the spirit."

"You come to my office."

"I don't think so, Barry. Let's try someplace a little more neutral, public."

"Well, like where?" Barry whined.

"How about someplace in, say, Chelsea?"

"Chelsea? Why Chel -- okay, where?"

"You pick the spot, Barry."

Exasperated, Barry said, "Just a second." Sam could picture him sweating like a pig. But he was not forgetting Barry was a real snake.

"Okay, there's a hotel on Eighth at 21st Street. A Chinese-Spanish, you name it, restaurant on the street level."

"I know the place."

"Tomorrow night at 9."

Too dark, thought Sam. He said, "Six."

"Six?"

"You'd rather meet on the stairs at the office again?" Sam sneered into the phone.

"Sonofabitch!" Then, "All right, 6. Tomorrow night at 6."

"Good boy, Barry. See you there."

Maybe Bill had been right. Sam hadn't known anything. But he was learning. He wouldn't be so stupid next time.

Chapter Twenty-Seven

After work Wednesday, Sam went straight home and started preparations for his encounter with Barry. He carefully applied a graying beard, smeared his face with enough grease to make it well street-worn and pulled on the tattered clothes. He'd already packed three guns in the old black bag with the broken handle. He had the two compact automatics -- the 9mm and the .40SW -- and the third was a slightly larger 9mm with a silencer. All three were nestled in wadded newspaper.

Finally, Sam pulled on an old raincoat and hat for leaving the building. These he would stash in the second plastic bag after he'd gone a few blocks.

By 5:15, Sam was shuffling along Eighth Avenue. He had watched a man the previous week meandering along West Broadway clutching his old bag, probably filled with all his possessions. Sam affected the man's manner as much as he could, but without the mutterings.

He approached the restaurant. It had broad windows across the front through which he could easily see the small room with high ceilings and suspended fluorescent lights washing down over a few scattered cheap tables and chairs. It was mainly a takeout place.

From where Sam stood across the street, he could see Barry

was not there. But he had a feeling he was nearby. Sam passed on, carefully observing.

Most people were hurrying home from work or hanging out with friends after a long day. A few, like himself, were displaced types, wandering, stopping occasionally to check a trash basket for food or other valuables. At 21st Sam turned left toward Ninth Avenue and shuffled toward a trash can he'd spied half a block away.

Then he crossed the street and headed back to Eighth. At a Korean deli near the corner stood a man pondering the bouquets of flowers out front. He'd been there when Sam first passed. It could be one of Barry's men. And there was sure to be another one nearby. Sam knew Barry and his ilk would work in packs, like wolves.

This time he crossed Eighth and then 21st and walked slowly past the restaurant, turning his head back and forth and muttering. There sat Barry near the counter with his back to the wall. Another man was at a table nearby, a blue and white seersucker jacket covering his broad shoulders. A little warm for that jacket, thought Sam. Unless you were hiding something. Sam stood at the end of the window where he had a good view, ostensibly fussing with his dilapidated bag. He checked every detail, Barry's clothes, his drawn face, his darting eyes. He hadn't been sure Barry would even show. Sam walked to the curb and leaned on a parking meter, an old man exhausted from his daily rounds in the street. Scratching his beard, he glanced back toward the deli. The man at the deli was staring like an alert fox, no longer interested in flowers.

Sam cleared his throat and spat in the street as the man's hand went under his jacket and Sam saw him pull out a cell phone as Sam started to turn away. Sam looked into the restaurant and saw the man in seersucker answer his phone, and immediately look out the front.

Sam turned before the man could catch his eye, but he saw the deli man hurrying across the street. Sam's heart pounded as he tried to retain his shuffling posture. Well, his mind quipped, this is what you came for.

Just as he reached the corner at 20th, sure he'd been made, Sam glanced back to his left, his hand inside the bag gripping the handle of the gun with the silencer.

For a second, he was caught totally off guard. The man from the deli had stopped an old woman pulling a two-wheeled cart with her groceries. She was bewildered as he spoke sternly, his hand under his jacket, apparently ready to pull out his gun. You putz, Sam chuckled to himself, you'd be dead already if she really was your quarry.

A sudden image of Bill bleeding on his bed rushed to Sam's mind. Careful, the alarm was saying. You are the one who must be cautious. Those men are, after all, professionals. Though he felt the urge to walk right up to the deli man and take him out, right there on the street, he resisted. Be smart, he told himself.

Instead, Sam shuffled across Eighth to a pay phone on the corner, a spot where he had full view of the restaurant.

Muttering and flipping the coin return open to keep people at a distance, Sam slipped in a quarter and dialed the number he'd memorized.

"Lee Lopez Restaurant."

"Is this Lee?" asked Sam.

"Hey," the man said, "you got an order? I'm busy."

"Yeah," Sam answered quickly. "A friend is picking up an

order. I need to give him one more thing. A Mr. Rabinowitz. Barry."

"Hey, buddy, this is a restaurant, not a paging service."

"Sure, sure, pal," Sam told him. "I'll tell Barry to give you an extra tip. Okay?"

With an exasperated pause, the man said, "All right. What's the name again?"

"Barry Rabinowitz. Brown blazer with a purple tie. You can't miss him."

"Yeah, I see him. Hang on. Hey, Rabinowitz!"

Barry must have been surprised; it took him a minute to get to the phone. "Yeah," was all he said.

"You brought a lot of help with you, Barry. It was just a meeting between you and me."

"What the --" Barry was snapping his fingers, beckoning at the corner out of Sam's view where the seersucker man sat.

"Before you call in the army, Barry, just let me assure you that if I wanted to, I'd already have put a nice red hole in that tasteless purple tie you're wearing. I'll call you later." Sam hung up the phone and slipped quickly to the shadows under the awning of a store, fussing with his bag.

He saw the two guards conferring at the entrance to the restaurant, Barry still holding the phone. Deciding to take the chance, Sam shuffled straight to 21st and crossed the street to the restaurant.

By the time he got across, Deli Man had checked up and down the walk, spying the phone where Sam had been, of course. But no one was there, so he signaled to Seersucker who motioned, in turn, to Barry. As Sam stepped onto the curb, Barry emerged, red-faced and boiling.

"Sonofabitch," Barry growled. "I'm gonna get that -- come on, let's get out of here!" They turned the corner. Sam waited a moment and followed.

It was half a block to where the driver waited with the black Lincoln Town Car. Seersucker opened the back door for Barry while Deli Man went to the other side. His hand tight on the grip of the gun in the bag, Sam acted quickly.

His gun jerked eagerly. Pamp! Pamp! Deli Man was dropping as he reached for the door on the other side. Quickly, Sam adjusted the bag as Seersucker was pulling his own gun from under his coat.

Pamp! Pamp! Pamp! The man sprawled backward before he could get his gun free, careening off the open front door of the car.

Pulling the automatic from the bag as he leapt into the front seat, Sam swung the long silencer muzzle into the driver's face. "Drive, asshole."

The handsome young man -- no more than 25 -- eased his right hand away from his belt where Sam assumed he had a gun, his eyes wide with surprise.

"Now!" Sam demanded.

"Pop?" said the driver. Sam flicked his eyes back at Barry.

"Do it," Barry told him. The car screeched away from the curb.

As they sped east, Sam looked behind them where half a dozen people had appeared at the corner. The action had taken less than a minute, but there was no time to spare now. They had to get away from the area.

"Where?"

"Let's just head for home," Sam snapped.

"But," the boy began.

"Right now, just carefully, two fingers, hand me that gun at your belt," he told the driver.

Slowly, the boy eased out the .38 and Sam grabbed it. He switched the silenced auto to his left hand to steady it on the driver and pointed the .38 at Barry. He could shoot him through the seat if he had to.

Turning to look at Barry, he affected a Gabby Hayes voice. "Bad business back there, Pop."

"Who --"

"Oh, please," said Sam, "don't start that again. I'm Gabby Hayes, I'm *Helen* Hayes. I'm your nightmare, Barry, remember?

"Call me Will, call me Jill," Sam was beginning to get into it. "But you doesn't has to call me Johnson!" He snickered and wheezed in Gabby Hayes tones.

"Right now," he said switching to his own voice, "we need to talk. Get to know one another, don't you think?" Barry obviously didn't know what to think. But Sam had to decide something quick.

"Taconic River Parkway," he said to the driver. "You know where that is, boy?"

"Yeah, I," the driver hesitated, glancing at the back seat in his mirror.

"Then just do it, son. What's your name anyway?"

"J-Jason."

"Jason!" Snicker, wheeze. "Well, isn't that just too trendy."

Barry's jaw was tightening as he leaned forward.

"Just sit back and relax, Pop," Sam said evenly. "No offense, Jason. That's a very nice name. No need to take it out on you just because your old man is treating me unkindly. And you have been a snake, Barry."

For several minutes there was only the droning of the car's engine and the passing traffic. Certainly neither Barry nor his son had anything to add.

They were just approaching FDR Drive on the east side of Manhattan and Sam was finally cooling down and getting his wits fully again. "Turn right at the next chance," he said.

"But you said --"

"I know, Jason," Sam indulged him, "but I've changed my mind. We'll just swing into Gramercy Park. See if you can find a place to park."

Jason nodded, with a quick look to the back seat via the mirror again.

"Barry," said Sam, "I'm very disappointed. All this violence has got to stop."

Barry's mouth remained closed and Sam continued. "You know, Will knew it was you who set him up." And with a steely look into Barry's eyes, he said, "He told me to get you."

Sam paused a minute, checking on Jason who had slowed the car. "What?"

"It's a parking place."

"Good. Make sure you've got plenty of room." Turning back to Barry, he said, "Like I said, get you. That's fine, Jason. Keep the engine running, both hands on the wheel. Where I can see them. Good boy."

Sam could see he was getting on Jason's nerves. He sort of enjoyed it in a sinister way, but he had nothing against the boy. He would try to ease up on him.

"We're businessmen, right, Barry?"

Barry grudgingly nodded.

"So, that leaves me with a quandary. Either I do business with you, or I honor my friend's dying request and," he paused ominously, "finish you."

Ever so slightly Barry's eyes widened. Jason was obviously agitated. He couldn't believe this was going to happen. Right here. On the street in Gramercy Park.

Outside, people went about their business, fetching dry cleaning, carrying home takeout. Life as usual. Staring unflinchingly at Barry, Sam cocked the hammer on the .38. "Well?"

Barry cringed, the muscles below his left eye jerking involuntarily. Perspiration was beading on his forehead.

"What's it going to be?" Sam pressed. "I don't really have much use for you personally. But every job has its channels." He was beginning to feel pretty chipper.

"What the heck," he interjected as Barry opened his mouth to speak. Again Barry cringed, thinking this was the end.

"Take it easy, Barry. We can do business, can't we?"

"Yeah," Barry said. He cleared his throat. "Sure, uh, Will. We can do business."

With a melodramatic sigh, Sam said, "Well, that is good, Barry. I was beginning to think you weren't interested." He eased the hammer down on the gun. Jason closed his eyes in relief.

As Sam grinned and nodded at Jason, Jason returned a weak smile. He hoped it was over. Even though the man next to him who looked very much like a street bum still pointed Jason's own gun at his father. His eyebrows raised in question.

Again Sam nodded. "Okay, Jason, let's drive."

"Where?"

"Head down to South Street Seaport."

"What?"

"Maybe we could get in some shopping," Sam said with a wink. "I could use some clothes, don't you think?"

Jason said, "Right," and pulled away from the curb, though his eyes told Sam he was thinking something else.

At 18th Street, Sam said, "Make a right."

"But you said --"

"Yeah, yeah. I'm a changeable guy. Make a right. And Barry, why don't you just ease your hand in your jacket and hand me your little gun."

"I, I don't have a gun," said Barry.

"Really?" Sam answered, amused.

"He doesn't, Mister," Jason hastily added. "Jack and -- they were the --"

"The gunmen?" Sam finished. "All right." Then to Barry, "Next time I'll shake you down, though. I don't trust you."

At Union Square, Sam said suddenly, "Drop me anywhere."

"What?" said Jason. This seemed to be practically the only word in his vocabulary, thought Sam.

"Pull to the curb. It's been a pleasure meeting with you, Barry. Oh, you too, Jason. I'll call you. We'll work out the details. Ciao," he said, jumping out of the car, the guns restored to the old black bag. He ducked quickly into the subway stairs.

The Lincoln sat idling, the passenger side door still open. Slowly, Barry leaned forward, straining to see the mysterious bum. But he was nowhere.

"Get the hell out of here," Barry said in a raspy voice.

Jason reached over and pulled the door shut and drove away.

CHAPTER TWENTY-EIGHT

Sam watched from the stairs as Barry's Lincoln left. Smiling and shaking his head, he thought, This was great! He felt a wave of remorse as he pictured shooting Barry's guards, but otherwise they would have shot me, he assured himself.

"Business," he said. A man in a coat and tie going down the stairs eyed him warily and Sam just cackled. Then he hurried up the stairs and rushed across the street to McDonald's.

To the counter attendant's surprise, the dirty-looking old street person before him ordered two Big Macs, slapping a $20 bill on the counter with a twinkle.

"You got a key for the bathroom, young man?"

"You don't need a key."

"Sonofagun. And I thought I had to buy these burgers to get in. Well, thanks," he said, grabbing up the bag. "Keep the change." And he bustled away.

Sam locked the bathroom door, set the burger bag on the sink and started peeling off the tattered clothes. In a few minutes, he had the entire costume stuffed in the plastic bag, leaving him in blue light-cotton pants and a dark blue T-shirt. He moved the burgers and scrubbed his hands and face. As he rubbed his damp fingers through his short hair, he stopped suddenly, staring at himself in the mirror.

"Damn!" he said. He grabbed his things and the burgers and hurried out.

"Seven o'clock," he muttered, snatching a peek at his watch as he stood at the top of the stairs to the subway. "Right." Sam charged down the stairs.

He caught the next N train to Times Square, switched to the No. 1 uptown and got off near the parking lot where he'd left the BMW. Fifteen minutes later he was cruising through the Midtown Tunnel to Queens.

He had opted for the Long Island Expressway and luck was with him. Most of the commute traffic had cleared so he reached Grand Central Parkway in no time, taking it south, merging with the Van Wyck down to the Belt Parkway. From there it was an easy ride to Rosedale.

He was sure Barry would be home already, because he had a feeling Barry was in a very big hurry. He rolled into Barry's neighborhood, down peaceful tree-lined streets. Finding Barry's street, he checked house numbers. Then he saw the tail of Barry's Lincoln.

Sam passed by slowly, scanning the area. The property was large for the neighborhood, with the driveway winding slightly past the house back under overhanging fir trees. Sam parked, dug through his bag for the simplest of disguises, glasses with a big nose. He added a gray plaid golf cap which he pulled down over his eyes.

He observed no one as he strolled along the sidewalk to Barry's house and with everything still quiet, he walked up the drive toward the Lincoln. He slipped back into the shrubs when he heard voices.

"What are you saying, Pop?"

"Dammit, Jason. This guy is crazy. There ain't gonna be another meeting. Don't worry about all your stuff. We'll arrange something. Now get some things packed and take your mother to Kennedy. Catch the next flight. I'll take the one right after that, meet you in Miami."

"But --"

"No 'buts.' This is no game! The guy is going to kill us."

"Are you sure? He --"

"I'm sure. I'm very sure. Now grab some stuff and get going. I want you out of here in 15 minutes. I'll be right behind you after I take care of a few things. Move! I'll explain the rest in Miami."

Barry watched as Jason disappeared into the house, then Barry jumped in the Lincoln, backed quickly out of the driveway and roared off down the street. Sam nodded. He wasn't surprised.

After a couple of minutes, when he was sure he wouldn't be noticed, he slipped down the drive and walked back to the BMW. He slowly drove away, back to the business area to find a phone.

"Joey?"

There was a pause, then, "Who is this?"

"I'm, I'm a good friend of Will's."

"Will?"

"Did some business for you. Through Barry. I'm sure you know Barry crossed him on the job last Thursday."

Silence. Then, "Keep talking. You got a name, Mister?"

"Will Junior. Sorry, sir, I mean no disrespect. I'm the one cleaned up Barry's guys at Carlo's. Also Rosano. But he'd already shot Will."

When Joey didn't reply, Sam continued, "I'm real sorry about Will. Real sorry. He's the one told me it was Barry. But like I said, I'm sure you already guessed it."

"I don't guess things, Mr. Junior. What's this got to do with me? I don't know you."

"I know you don't, Mr. Napoli. But I wouldn't have this number unless I knew Will real well, would I?"

"You're not telling me anything so far," answered Joey.

"Well, let me tell you this. Barry's on his way out of town. Now I want to continue business with you. Pick up where Will left off. It's the least I could do for him. Barry'd already double-crossed Will once before last week, but when I tried to tell him I was taking over Will's work --"

"You what?" Joey laughed.

"That's right. Anyway, there's not much time. Like I said, I want to work with *you*. Barry's just an impediment."

"An impediment," Joey repeated.

"Yes, sir. If you'd have your people check on it, check on Barry, you'll see I'm telling you straight. All I'm saying is, you say the word and I'll deliver Barry to you. On a plate. Will asked me to get him."

Again Joey chuckled. "And you propose to?"

"I'll call you back in 15 minutes. Half hour if you need it to check on Barry's hurried vacation. And when I call, you say the word, I'll stop the slime. This is to show my good faith, Mr. Napoli. I know you had nothing to do with setting Will up."

"Uh-huh. Fifteen minutes?"

"Or 30 if you --"

"Yeah, right. Okay, Junior. You make that call in 15 minutes. We'll talk."

"Yes, sir."

"And get a name."

"Yes, sir. Call you at 8:15." Sam hung up.

CHAPTER TWENTY-NINE

Sam drove around for a few minutes, deciding to make the next call from a different pay phone. He might as well practice being careful.

He stopped at a 7-11 for a Dr Pepper, checked his watch and made the call.

"You got a name?"

"Rob," said Sam.

"Got a last name?"

"Yeah. Samson."

"Is that Rob for Robert?"

"Uh, yes, sir."

"Okay, Rob for Robert. As you said, Barry's not answering. Barry's wife and kid --"

"Jason."

"Don't interrupt. Right, Jason. They were spotted over at Kennedy."

"He told them to take the next plane to Miami," Sam informed Napoli.

"You seem to know a lot about this."

"Yes, sir. I was standing in the bushes outside his house when he told Jason."

"First-name basis with everyone, you are," said Joey gruffly.

"No, Mr. Napoli. But when I tried to meet with Barry

earlier this evening, I had to take out his guards."

"You what?"

"Eliminated his guards. They were going to kill me. There was no doubt. I took a ride with Barry. And that's when I found out his son, Jason, is his driver."

There was silence on the other end of the phone. Sam began to think he'd been disconnected.

"Mr. Napoli?"

"Hang on, Samson."

Sam waited.

A police car pulled into the 7-11, parking at the other end. One of the officers got out and headed into the store, carefully eyeing the BMW M5. Sam watched out of the corner of his eye.

"All right, Samson."

"Yes, Mr. Napoli."

"You seem to know a lot about Barry's business."

"No, sir. I was just in the right place at the right time. I had a feeling after our meeting earlier that Barry was about to run. So I tracked him to his house."

"Yeah. And you'd like to take care of Barry and make some points with me." It was not a question.

"Yes, sir. If you'd like."

"And what if I don't like?"

Sam hadn't thought of that. He was so sure Joey would not like to hear Barry was leaving town. He said, "Then I don't. I leave it."

Napoli paused and said, "That's the right answer."

Sam breathed a silent sigh of relief. Which was tempered slightly as the cop came out of the 7-11 carrying a bag and stopped to examine the BMW again. He looked momentarily at Sam, then went over and got in the squad car.

"Ding, ding," went the phone. "Please deposit 60 cents for another five minutes."

Damn! thought Sam. What next? He fished in his pocket and dropped in the coins.

"Professional," quipped Joey.

"I want to be near my work," Sam said without thinking. He wished he'd thought first.

But Joey just laughed. "Okay, Mr. Professional, you're right. I don't want Barry leaving town without telling. What are you going to do about it?"

"I'll deliver him. Where you say and however you say."

"I don't need to talk to him."

"Fine with me," said Sam coldly. "I owe him. But you will want to know it's handled. I can deliver him -- what's left -- in his car, maybe. Wherever you want."

"I'll read about it in the papers, Mr. Samson. Call me." Click.

Sam held the phone a second, letting it all soak in. Joey went for it. Sam was thrilled!

He hung up the phone and turned. The squad car was gone. The cops must have been just admiring his M5. Sam jumped in and went back to Barry's.

The lights were still on when Sam drove past the house. Again he stopped up the street, parking beneath a huge ginkgo tree that hung down almost to the ground. He slipped on the nose-glasses and cap again and walked to Barry's, taking his bag with him this time.

He didn't have to wait in the bushes for long. The tires squealed as Barry swerved into the driveway, but he pulled past the house, past Sam. Sam was ready as Barry walked back toward him.

"Good evening, Barry," said Sam as Barry reached for the door. "Going someplace?"

"What?" Barry jumped, then stood stiffly, his back still to Sam.

"Joey wasn't too happy about your unannounced departure," Sam began.

Barry whirled around, "You!" he screamed. Then, "Aarrrghh!" Before Sam knew it, Barry had pulled out a revolver. "Die in hell, you monster!" he yelled as he fired.

Sam reacted quickly. Pamp! Pamp, pamp! he fired as the branch next to his right ear snapped when a bullet whizzed by.

Barry was wide-eyed, his body nailed to the wall next to the door, his gun held at an awkward angle. He looked like some sort of urban scarecrow. Then with an odd gurgle, he slid down into a heap on the steps.

Sam stood frozen a moment. He was charged up all over, but he felt particularly hot on the right side of his face. Reaching up, he touched his ear.

"Ouch." He held bloody fingers before his face.

Sam pulled one of the rags from his bag, touched his ear again to make sure it was all there and then held the rag to the side of his face.

It's nothing, he told himself. Barry's the one who's in trouble. Big mistake, Barry.

But it's just done sooner, he thought. Now what?

Well, Joey had said he would read about it. So fine, that's it.

Sam listened. The neighborhood was so damn quiet. He edged down the driveway in the cover of the shrubs. A couple of lights were on at houses that weren't earlier. But maybe it was nothing. However, he couldn't hang around.

Sam looked both ways again, then slipped down to the sidewalk and walked slowly to his car. After he got in he sat a minute longer and, seeing and hearing nothing, he drove off.

He'd done it. He'd taken care of Barry.

You're welcome, Bill.

Chapter Thirty

When the alarm woke him, Sam was disoriented. He didn't even realize where he was. Then he turned the radio off, stepped out of bed and headed for the shower.

He had been so ebullient the night before that he'd driven around for hours, first hitting the Southern State Parkway and heading east until it ended and then turning west through quaint Long Island villages. Finally, he filled up with gas and veered north, taking the expressway back to Manhattan. It was 1:30 before he was settled down enough to go to sleep.

This morning Sam had to spend so long in the shower waking up that he decided to pass on his run. He would take the long walk down to the office instead. He didn't hurry but was still out the door by 6:45.

It was another wonderful day. Sam strolled along the quiet streets, through the Village, then down Greenwich toward Canal. There was hardly any traffic. Only a large dark limo cruising southward.

The car stopped at the curb just past him.

Two men emerged. The one at the door nearest him had on a snug black suit, black shirt and dark sunglasses.

"Get in," he told Sam.

"But --" Sam began to panic.

"Mr. Robbins," said the man on the other side across the top of the car, "please step in. Mr. Napoli would like a word with you."

What? Sam's brain screamed. This was not what he'd expected. "But I have to get to work," he bumbled.

"You'll be late," came a voice from inside the car. Sam recognized that voice.

As Sam entered the car, Joey Napoli smiled at him. "Have a seat, Mr. Robbins," he motioned.

Sam stared with his mouth agape and sat opposite Napoli. The doors closed and the car began to move.

"So, we meet at last," Napoli chuckled.

"But," Sam stuttered.

"You said that several times. What happened to the professional Mr. Samson I spoke with last night? Cat got your tongue?"

A flash of anger swept over Sam. "I wasn't expecting to get together so soon," he snapped.

"Ha ha. That's more like it," Joey laughed, slapping his thigh with a large gnarled hand draped with rings. Then he leaned forward and confided, "You really didn't expect me not to find out all about you, did you?"

Sam sighed, arching his eyebrows. "No. Of course not," he admitted. "So is this where I buy it?"

"Hah, hah, hah!" laughed Joey again. The others joined in. "You see too many movies, son."

Flushed with embarrassment, Sam shot his eyes from one to the other.

"But that's what I like about you. You're funny." Joey leaned toward him. "And you've got a lot of spunk. So we caught you with your pants down. Don't let it get you."

"Right," Sam agreed. "Look, Barry's --"

"I read the early edition, Sam. You don't mind if I call you Sam, do you?"

"N-no, of course not."

"You're right, Sam. You did just what you said. And, no, we're not here to finish you off, too. I just want to say, thanks." He held out his hand.

Awkwardly, Sam shook hands.

"Will was something special, Sam. And I think you really were his friend."

"Yes. Thank you, sir. I was."

The car had stopped. Sam's eyes shifted as he worried what was happening.

The door opened and the same man stood there.

"You'll be hearing from us," Napoli told him. "Don't worry. You're right back where we picked you up."

As Sam stepped out, he was bewildered, awed. Finally, he found his tongue. "Thanks, Mr. Napoli. I won't let you down."

"No, you won't," said Napoli.

Sam stood watching the car drive off, caught in the cloud of his new life. It would never be the same again, he thought.

When the car disappeared around the corner, Sam continued on toward work.

In a nondescript beige Ford parked at the corner a block to the north sat Detective Jackson Carter. He screwed up his forehead as he twisted his lower lip with the fingers of his right hand. For a brief moment he sat frozen, then, shaking his head, he slipped the car in gear and headed east. He didn't have any real evidence of a connection yet. But he wasn't finished with Sam Robbins.

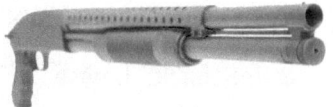

ACKNOWLEDGMENTS

For their enthusiastic feedback, I wish to thank Bill Cryer, Diane McClure, my sons Dimic and Dylan Robertson, and former colleagues Greg Reznikov and Jack Tadej.

And for their continuing inspiration, writer friends H.J. Cummins, Blake Green, Barbara Falconer Newhall and Jon Newhall, and Anne Raver.

Additional thanks to editor Aviva Layton and publisher Lara Reznik.

Finally, special thanks to my number one editor, Ginger Rothé.

About the Author

Ron G. Robertson worked in one of the towers in downtown Manhattan where he shared a peregrine falcon's view of the city and walked the same stairs as his protagonist. He now lives and writes in Austin, Texas.